The Bon Air Boys Adventures Series

Footprints In The Attic

By

GREG W. GOLDEN

This book is not intended to endorse or promote any of the activities by the characters contained therein. Any similarity between locations or these characters to actual places or those persons living or dead is coincidental. This is a fictional story.

For my grandchildren
Grant, Iris, Ellie, and Violet
and with special thanks to
my wife Debbie for being my
first and best sounding board and editor

About The Author

Greg Golden grew up in middle America, the youngest of three children and the only son of a pastor. Greg's love for literature was first demonstrated when at the age of ten he ran out of the entire library of Hardy Boys books available to read, and he wrote one for himself.

After college, his career path took him to Mobile, Alabama, where he met and married Debbie. There they raised two sons, and those sons and wives have given them numerous grandchildren—the newest loves and diversions in their lives.

Greg is an ordained minister, and he frequently mentors those who come across his path seeking encouragement and guidance.

Contents

Everyone turned to see for themselves what Kate had noticed. A pickup truck behind them was rapidly closing the distance to their sedan. The person driving was having trouble controlling his vehicle. He veered left and right and, at times, crossed into the oncoming traffic lane. The trailer that the truck was towing teetered and leaned dangerously whenever the driver tried to return to his lane. A blind curve was just ahead. Kate immediately realized that the driver had two choices— and both had bad outcomes.

"Brace yourselves because he's not stopping!" Kate yelled to the boys. "He's either going to pass us or hit us!

From *"Footprints In The Attic"*

Footprints
In The
Attic

Chapter 1

Frank Whidden leaned back on his stool, drew in a deep breath, and pushed both fists over his head in a gesture of victory. He smiled to himself and whispered aloud, "*Yessssss!* I *did* it, and *it works!*"

It didn't matter that the only other living thing in the basement nearby was Frank's dog, asleep on the floor a few feet away. "Duke, look at it!" he said.

Duke, the Whidden's four-year-old sable and white collie, a Lassie look-alike, raised his head when he heard his name. "Isn't it beautiful?" Frank said aloud as he ran his fingers around the edge of the two-foot-wide metal bowl. Duke didn't seem to have the same appreciation for the device as his master because, after a few seconds, he lowered his head to the concrete floor, took a deep breath, and closed his eyes.

Frank smiled to himself, then rolled the stool away from his workbench and stood.

"*Is somebody down there with you?*" The voice from the doorway at the top of the basement belonged to Frank's sister Kate. She was five years older than him and a sophomore at the community college.

"Nope, it's just Duke and me. But come see what I made, Kate!"

She walked down the stairs and crossed the basement to her brother. Kate had kind, blue-green eyes and light brown hair. She was Frank's only sibling

11

and was, without question, his biggest fan. Maybe their age difference was why they respected each other and got along so well. But whatever the reason, as sister and brother, it was clear to everyone who knew them that they were surprisingly good friends.

"Okay, *w-h-a-t exactly* am I looking at?" Kate asked. "And does Dad know that you have the lid from his bar-b-que grill down here?"

Frank's smile turned into a mischievous grin. "Well, I'm only borrowing it for now, and I'll give it back— eventually! But just look at it, Kate! It will revolutionize the way our football games sound over the campus radio station! Can't you just picture me standing on the sidelines? When I point this at the players on the field, I'll be able to pick up everything the guys in the huddle say. That'll make it *much* more interesting for the people who listen to our football games on the radio when they can't make it out to the stadium!"

"I'll take your word for it," Kate said. She raised one eyebrow and pretended to smile. "It looks good—I guess." She turned away, took a step, then stopped and faced Frank again. "Oh, the reason I came down here was to tell you that Griff called on the phone for you just before I heard your voice in the basement. It had been so quiet all afternoon I didn't realize you were home." As she headed for the stairs again, a thought struck her. "Um, would that invention of yours work for bird calls, too?"

"*Of course*, Kate!" he replied with the playful tone he sometimes used to imply that *everyone* should know that answer. "It's a parabolic reflector. It gathers whatever sounds are directly in front of it and focuses them into this microphone." He pointed to the slim, silver-colored device aimed at the center of the metal bowl that was held in place by three twisted coat hanger wires. "To be honest, I haven't actually tested it in the *outside* world—only here in the basement. But I am positive it will work to pick up any sound. The principle is foolproof!"

"The reason I asked," Kate continued, "is because, for my zoology course, I have to do a project about the types of birds found in our area and the calls they make. If you could bring your parasol and go with me..."

Frank stiffened and interrupted her. "It's a parabolic, *par-a-BOL-ic* reflector, Kate!"

"Yes, that's what I meant! If you would bring that thing and go with me tomorrow after church, I'm planning a trip to the nature preserve. I think our dad's... I, I mean, your invention will be a huge help to me with my project!"

"I can do it, Sis. And as a bonus, I will also record all of the bird calls on my trusty, battery-powered tape recorder! I'll throw that in for *free* just because you're my sister." He tilted his head slightly and winked one eye. Frank pointed to the device on the workbench. "But do *not* tell your college friends about this, because then everyone will be calling here asking for my help!"

Kate made a click-click sound with her tongue, winked back at him, and raised a thumb. "It's a deal," she said as she climbed the steps and disappeared from view.

"Duke, it looks like Kate and you and I are going to spend some time in the great outdoors tomorrow."

Duke raised his head again. He rose to his feet,

stretched, shook himself from head to tail, and followed Frank up the stairs.

·······

"Breaker, breaker, are either of you guys on your radios?" Frank spoke into his walkie-talkie and then released the transmit button. It was a minute past 8:00 PM, the usual time each evening for Frank, Griff, and Chase to switch on their two-way radios and converse from their bedrooms.

The three boys, best friends for as long as they could remember, lived within a few blocks of each other in the Bon Air Village neighborhood near Lewisville's eastern town limits. Each of their families treated the other two boys like adopted sons, and they regularly ate meals at their friends' tables. And although their personalities were different, each boy respected the traits of the others.

You rarely saw just one of them around town. They played sports, hiked trails, attended church, studied for exams, and camped together. Usually, they traveled as a trio on foot or atop their bicycles in their constant crisscrossing through and around Lewisville, the largest town in Jeffers County.

Griff's dad was a year and a half into his third term as the elected Sheriff. Chase's father ran the family's hardware store near the town square along Main Street. And Frank's dad owned an insurance agency a block west of City Hall. Their mothers were all active volunteers in their school, at church, and with various civic groups in town.

"You got me!" The voice that crackled loudly through Frank's radio speaker was Chase's. He was the youngest of the three friends, but only by two months. Chase was also the self-appointed jokester and comedian among them.

"I'm here!" Griff said and then added, "What've you guys been up to today?"

The conversation that followed was typical for them in their nightly two-way radio visits. The discussion consisted of what had taken place in their lives on that day—mostly meaningless small talk about nothing of real importance.

More often than not, the three of them would have spent at least half of a Saturday together working on a community cleanup project, sorting clothing for their church's free food and clothes distribution, or serving as volunteer leaders for the Cub Scouts of local Troop 54. When the weather cooperated or on summer days, they might be found mowing lawns, weeding flowerbeds, or raking leaves for their part-time business venture *The Yard Guys*. And usually, a ball—a football, baseball, basketball, or soccer ball—would be involved in their free time. On this Saturday, however, each of them started the morning at his breakfast table and then stayed around his own home—to the surprise and delight of all their parents.

Chase replied to Griff's question first. "Matt and I helped our dad clean out the garage. Then after lunch, we tossed a Frisbee around the backyard until it was time for supper. We made up a little game with the disc and threw it at different targets in the yard—kinda like golf holes."

Frank spoke next. "My dad and I helped Mr. Rigsby move some furniture in his house, and then I spent the rest of the afternoon working on my newest project, a parabolic microphone. I'm going to get the chance to put it to a real test tomorrow when Kate and I go to the nature preserve to check out some of the birds there."

"That sounds very cool, Frank. I'm impressed! I remember that you were talking about building it. I'd love to see it in operation sometime," Griff said.

"We'll be heading there after lunch to find and identify some birds. Why don't you two come here—say around 1:30—and ride there with us?" Frank offered. "I'll be bringing Duke along for the outing, too."

"That sounds like a lot of fun," Chase said. "About your parabolic microphone...what did you use for the main part—the reflector bowl?"

"I actually had the rather brilliant idea to borrow the lid from my dad's bar-b-que grill," Frank said. "It's the right shape, and there's already a handle built in to it. I added three little spring-loaded clamps to attach the support wires—some twisted coat hangers—to hold the microphone in place. When I plug all of that into my portable tape recorder and add a pair of headphones, I'm betting that I can hear sounds from fifty yards away! I tested it on a cricket in the corner of the basement. We'll find out how well it works outdoors when we go tomorrow."

"I've been past that preserve place all of my life," Chase said, "but I don't think I've ever been inside it."

Griff quickly replied. "You must have forgotten because you *have* been there, Chase. We *all* have! It was where our fourth-grade class went for the spring field trip."

Frank jumped into the discussion and added, "That's right! And that's the same place where I got tangled up in some poison ivy. I've never itched so much in my whole life!"

"This time, keep your hands in your pockets and don't wander off the path," Chase suggested, which caused everyone to laugh.

"I'm going to have to sign off now," Griff told the others. "My little brother keeps knocking on my door. During supper, Geoff dared me to play him in a one-on-one ping-pong tournament. I need to win a few games to protect my title as the 'King of Ping.' I'll see you two at church in the morning!"

Frank and Chase acknowledged their friend's challenge, wished him luck, and said goodbyes, making their favorite walkie-talkie channel quiet once again.

·······

During Sunday lunch at the Whiddens' house, Frank informed Kate that he had invited his two buddies to tag along. "And I think that Duke would like the chance to be outdoors with us and get some exercise."

"It's all fine with me, but keep in mind that this is a high fence preserve, and you'll need to keep Duke on a leash. It's a *huge* place—over six hundred acres—and it is a privilege for us to go onto the property."

Frank's expression changed to a look of confusion when Kate said the words *"high fence preserve."* His dad noticed the question mark on his face.

"Son, a high fence preserve is a great description

of exactly what it is. A twelve-foot-tall fence surrounds the entire property, and the entry is controlled with a locked gate. All of that is in place to keep the preserve's animals *in* and keep the wild predators *out*. A caretaker lives next to the grounds, and there are scores of deer—some of them very valuable—along with some exotic animals that he watches out for. Mr. Rigsby owns the land. I thought you knew all of that."

Frank stopped shoveling the spaghetti, salad, and garlic bread into his mouth, shrugged his shoulders, and said, "I must have forgotten."

....

By 1:15, Frank and his dad had cleared the table, washed the dishes, and put them away. At 1:30, Chase's signature knock sounded on the back door. Mr. Whidden greeted Chase and Griff as Frank tried to restrain his very excited collie, Duke.

"Here, hold on to this, please," he said to Chase as he passed the leash's hand strap to his friend. "I need to go to the basement and get my parabolic dish and the tape recorder."

Kate appeared in the kitchen doorway with a small canvas bag slung on her shoulder and a three-ring binder in her hand. Her binoculars hung on a sturdy strap around her neck. "Guys, we can go ahead and get in the car and wait for Frank there."

They followed her outside and left the door ajar for Frank. The three of them and Frank's dog began to get settled in Kate's mother's sedan. Griff and Chase dropped into the back seats with Duke between them, while Kate opened the trunk for Frank's things. In another moment, her brother appeared in the kitchen doorway and made his way down the porch steps. Frank's tape recorder hung from a strap over one shoulder. He wore the headphones around his neck, and he held on to his prized invention using both hands.

When everything was securely in the trunk, Frank slid into the front passenger seat and tightened his seat belt.

Kate turned toward Griff and Chase. "I'm glad that you guys coul join us. And you, too, Duke. This place is full of prized, even some rare wildlife. But I can't guarantee what, if anything, we'll see." Kate adjusted the rearview mirror, placed the car into reverse, and continued speaking as the trip began. "Let's just plan to stay close to each other. And I'd be grateful if you'll help me spot some different species of birds. The more types I can identify, the better my grade will be for this zoology project."

Their destination was four miles south of Lewisville—less than ten minutes away by car.

"I've never heard Mr. Rigsby talk about this place. Has he owned it for a long time?" Frank asked Kate.

"As I understand him, it was land that his wife's family had owned for several generations. She inherited it from her parents around forty or fifty years ago. Then when she died, it became his property. Mr. Rigsby hasn't been actively involved with it except to be sure that the caretaker, who is one of his wife's nephews, has the things he needs to keep it running."

Two miles into their trip, all of them heard a siren,

and within several more seconds, an ambulance, with red lights flashing behind the grill and on the roof, was only a few car lengths behind Kate. She slowed and steered as far to the edge of the road as she could to make room for the emergency vehicle. It quickly passed them and was soon out of view.

Griff broke the silence and spoke from the rear seat. "I'll bet it's heading to Covington Community Hospital. I could see a paramedic through the back window, and he was leaning over someone in the back." He paused for a few seconds and then said thoughtfully, "That's a tough way for things to go on somebody's Sunday afternoon."

After a few more miles, Kate pulled on her turn signal lever and pointed her passengers' attention to an unmarked gravel road. "This is it. The driveway is about a half-mile long, and then we'll reach the caretaker's house next to the main gate."

Duke had begun the trip seated upright between Griff and Chase, taking in the sights around them. After the first mile, however, he made himself comfortable and rested his head on Griff's leg. Once they reached the gravel driveway and Duke heard the noise it made under the car's tires, the collie rose to his feet sensing he was about to experience something new. When they stopped at the gate, Kate and Frank got out of the car to check in with the caretaker. During that time, it was all that Chase could do to keep Duke from jumping out of a backseat window!

The two boys and Duke watched from the car as a large man with thinning hair mopped sweat from his face onto a blue bandana as he walked to the gate. At the same time, Kate and Frank returned to their seats. The man took a ring of keys from a belt clip, opened a padlock, and removed the chain from the tall metal gate. The man shoved the left half of it open and then pushed the other side of the gate until the gravel driveway was clear for them to pass through. "Stay on the path," he reminded them with a stern voice.

Once they were away from the entrance, Frank spoke. "Mr. Denton told me that he would close the gate behind us but wouldn't lock it. We will just need to honk our horn to get out when we are ready to leave," he said over his shoulder to his friends.

Kate cautiously drove ahead another quarter of a mile until the narrow driveway ended. She parked in a clearing large enough to hold a half-dozen cars. "This is as far as we can go. For the rest of our time here, we'll be on foot. They don't allow vehicles anywhere on the grounds past this point."

Duke climbed onto Griff's lap. The swishing of his fluffy tail in Griff's face showed everyone his excitement to finally get out of the car. When they exited the vehicle and closed the four doors, they gathered by the rear of the sedan. Kate unlocked the trunk, and Frank removed his invention and slung the tape recorder strap across one shoulder. His sister picked up her things.

Duke tested the strength of Griff's grip on the retractable leash as he sniffed the ground. "He's found the scent of an animal! I think he'd much rather run around than have me hold on to him," Griff observed.

"That leash can roll out about fifteen feet, so he'll have plenty of freedom to explore," Frank replied.

The four of them and Duke strolled away from the

car and walked about five hundred feet into the mature forest of pine, spruce, fir, and hemlock trees.

"Look at that buck rub!" Chase exclaimed as he pointed to a pine tree. "You can see where some deer antlers have scraped the bark off this one! He must have been marking his territory."

Birds flitted overhead and chirped their calls that sounded to the boys like the words *bob-white, jink denk te-e-e-e,* and *pidaro pidaro pidaro.* Something unseen scurried behind them in the leaves and pine straw layers that formed a brownish blanket almost everywhere. Kate stopped walking, reached into her shoulder bag, and retrieved her *Field Guide Book of Birds.* In it were color photos and descriptions of the sounds the birds made to help the group identify the many species around Lewisville.

Frank lifted and placed the headphones over his ears. He then switched on the tape machine and pressed RECORD. Frank pointed the bowl-shaped device upward toward a branch holding several birds, listened for a moment, and then, wearing a wide grin, looked at Kate and his friends. "It sounds like they are only two feet away! It's *awesome*! I can hear *everything*!"

They continued walking toward a clearing about fifty yards away. Frank gripped the parabolic bowl with both hands and aimed it in different directions to the left and right. At times he stopped and adjusted its position by just a few degrees. *"This thing is just amazing!"* he exclaimed. "See that squirrel over there?" Chase and Griff strained their gaze in the direction Frank had motioned, but they saw nothing. Kate lifted her binoculars and focused on the distant animal. "He's nibbling on a nut or some sort of food. I can hear it SO clearly!"

"Let's keep moving, guys, and try to find some birds for me, okay?" Kate pleaded.

At the edge of the clearing, Kate spied an Eastern Bluebird perched on a low branch across the open area. The four of them stayed beneath the canopy of tree branches when Kate cautioned, "We don't want to frighten away any of the wildlife."

She pointed to her left. "Frank, try to get some sounds recorded onto tape from that one," Kate urged.

Frank aimed the bowl with its microphone at the bird, checked that the tape recorder levels were good, and gave his sister a smile and a thumbs up. "It's perfect! *You* probably can't hear anything from this far away, but *I'm* getting all of it captured onto tape. You're going to *love* this!" Frank said with a smile.

At that moment, the bird jumped off the branch into the air, flitted toward the sky, then flew across the open space and beyond the line of trees.

They walked another hundred feet along the edge of the clearing. Kate recognized a Brown-headed Cowbird and placed a checkmark by that species on her list. They waited in the area as more birds came and went. Frank recorded the sounds made by each one of them. Griff and Chase took turns holding Duke's leash and letting him sniff the ground for scents left by rabbits, deer, and who knows what else.

In the half-hour that followed, Kate pointed out several more types of birds. Frank recorded their unique whistles, chirps, and calls while she placed checkmarks by their names on her list.

Then, while they waited to spy the next bird, Frank slowly swept the parabolic bowl device along the horizon to his right and scanned past the low branches. He suddenly froze! His eyes widened, and his shoulders tensed. Frank put one finger to his lips, motioning for everyone to be quiet. After a moment of listening, he lowered the microphone and slipped the headphones away from his ears.

"Guys, I just heard two men talking. I can't see anyone across the clearing which must mean they are standing back among the trees. What they were saying sounded to me like they were discussing a plan to steal something—something pretty valuable!" Frank tilted his tape recorder to better see the rotating tape reels through the window of the machine's cover. The reels were no longer turning. He pushed the STOP button with a discouraged sigh, realizing that the battery power had run out.

Frank felt confident that he had successfully recorded the squirrel, the first bluebird, and most of the other birds; but he couldn't be sure whether or not his tape machine had captured the men's conversation from among the distant trees. He had no way to tell when it had stopped operating, so he wouldn't know what he had captured—if anything—until after they returned to town and he installed new batteries.

Chapter 2

Griff could see Frank's disappointment, and he placed an arm across his friend's shoulders. "I'll bet you got everything that Kate needed—and maybe even those men's voices, too."

Kate reached a hand toward her brother and touched Frank's arm. "Let's call it a day and head home, guys."

The four of them turned and began to walk toward their car parked a hundred yards away at the far end of the clearing. Suddenly they heard a rustling of hooves in the leaves, and they saw a small deer trot into the sunlight. The animal paused for a few seconds and turned her head toward the group. Then she galloped across the meadow toward the far side, playfully kicking her hind feet high into the air. Duke strained at his leash, yelped loudly, and then pulled with all of his might. Chase gripped the strap with both hands, but the retractable cord gave way with a snap. In only an instant, Frank's dog was in pursuit of the deer and out of sight among the distant trees!

Chase dropped what remained of the broken leash without saying a word, and he and Griff dashed after the collie, whistling and yelling Duke's name as they ran.

Frank was too stunned by what had just happened to react. He lowered the parabolic bowl to his side as he watched his friends sprint to the place where the deer and Duke had entered the distant line of trees.

"Why don't you stay here, Frank. I'm sure they'll find him. Don't worry," Kate said encouragingly. "Let's keep on walking to the car. They're bound to figure out that we went there when they come back with Duke."

They continued walking and soon reached the parked sedan. Kate unlocked the trunk, and Frank stowed the metal bowl. He laid his tape recorder and headphones on the passenger seat and returned to the rear of the car. Kate put her things, except for the binoculars, into the trunk. Then she closed the lid and they waited.

Five minutes passed. Frank checked his wristwatch. Ten minutes went by.

"There's a fence around the entire preserve, Frank. He really can't get *completely* away," Kate said.

After fifteen minutes, his hopes had faded, and he prepared himself for the likelihood that Duke wouldn't be going home with them.

"How big is this place, anyway?" Frank asked.

"I think it's over seven hundred acres—about a square mile. It's big, all right, but..."

Far in the distance, Griff and Chase stepped through the border of trees and into the meadow. Frank lifted the binoculars and spotted his friends trudging toward the car. Duke was not with them. Frank lowered the field glasses and turned away from his sister as tears began to fill his eyes

......

Their car slowly approached the closed gate. Kate came to a stop and then tapped once on her horn. The caretaker, who was conversing at the driver's window of a parked car, looked at Kate through the gate and acknowledged them with a wave of one hand. After a moment, he walked briskly to the closed gate and pulled both halves of it open. Kate drove forward and steered to the right side of the narrow driveway to make room for the other vehicle. She parked, left the engine idling, but exited the car. Kate opened the trunk, and took a notepad and pen from her purse. The three boys waited several minutes in silence for her to return.

Once Kate was behind the wheel again, she spoke to her three passengers in the most encouraging voice she could find under the circumstances. "The driver of that car is Patrick Wilson, a soldier who is stationed at Fort Everett a little bit southwest of here. Mr. Denton lets him come and hike in the preserve on weekends when he can leave the base. I told him about our dog running off and asked if he would be on the lookout for him. I gave him our information in case he finds Duke."

"That's *great!*" Griff said excitedly from the back seat.

Trying to sound more confident than he actually was, Chase spoke up. "I'm going to pray right now that that man finds him and calls you! Kate, don't start driving yet. Bow your heads, guys. *God, you know exactly where Duke is because you see and know everything. Please let Mr. Wilson find him and get him back to us soon! Amen.*"

· · · · · · ·

Once they had arrived at the Whiddens' home, Frank took his parabolic bowl to the basement workbench.

27

When he returned, the three friends climbed the steps together and gathered in his bedroom around the desk. He unboxed four new D-sized batteries and pressed them into their slots in the rear compartment of his portable tape recorder. After closing the plastic cover, he turned the device over and switched it on. The audio level meters on the front glowed, and Frank rewound several minutes of recorded tape. He adjusted the volume control to three-quarters and pressed PLAY. Griff and Chase leaned forward, anxious to hear from the speaker whatever Frank's device had captured.

The clear sounds of birds chirping, dragonfly wings buzzing, and the gentle rustling of treetop leaves filled the room. As the tiny reels of tape on the recorder slowly turned, Frank listened intently, thinking about what he had focused on during those moments back in the nature preserve. "I was trying to get the dish pointed so that the voices were clearest," Frank explained to his friends.

No one in the room spoke, but in another thirty seconds, the speaker on the recorder blared the two men's words. One voice had a low pitch, and the other was higher.

"...there shouldn't be anyone around at that time of day," the man with the higher voice said. The first part of his sentence was not clear enough to understand.

"I know my way around the place, so it won't matter if it's dark or not. I won't need any kind of light," boomed the low voice.

The higher voiced man urged the other one, "Just be sure we notice the spot where we go in so we can get out of there fast. We'll make a lot more do-re-mi—

28

maybe even twice as much—if we get the goods and nothing's been damaged."

"Yeah, I bet we can get a big load this time! It's going to be some kinda huge payday!" said the man with the deep voice.

"So, when will this all..."

The tape reels continued to turn, but the speaker became silent.

"That has to be when the batteries went dead," Frank said. He let his tape recorder play for another fifteen seconds hoping for more words from the men. But when they heard nothing more, he pressed STOP and looked at his friends.

"Do you remember anything else those men said before they stopped talking?" Griff asked. *"Anything at all?"*

"The only other word that stuck out to me was the word *fair*—something about *fair*," Frank replied.

Chase stepped away and breathed a low whistle. "This sounds *serious*, guys. We *gotta* tell someone!"

"Now, hold on for a second," Griff said. "I think you might be jumping to a conclusion over what could be a perfectly..." His voice trailed off. Hesitating, he said, "It could have been just any random conversation."

"Let's think about this logically," Frank said. He pulled open a desk drawer and located a pencil. Frank pushed his tape recorder aside and wrote the number *"1"* along the left margin. "What do we know for sure?" he asked.

At that moment, Mr. Whidden tapped urgently on Frank's door and pushed it open. "Boys, I hate to interrupt, but I thought you'd want to know. Mr.

Rigsby was taken to the hospital a couple of hours ago." He looked at Frank. "Your mom and I just now learned about it from a neighbor of his. We are getting ready to drive down to Covington to check on him. I don't know how long we'll be away. Kate wants to ride with us. Do you want to go, too."

"I do, Dad, but I've been hoping that the man Kate talked to when we were leaving the preserve would call here. I would hate to miss him if he did. When you see Mr. Rigsby, please tell him that I'll be praying for him. I can fix myself something for supper."

Leonard Rigsby lived in one of Lewisville's largest and most distinctive houses. It was a three-story brick structure with a broad porch and white columns across the front entrance. Although he was not a relative of the Whiddens, Frank's dad grew up knowing Mr. Rigsby as a sort of substitute grandfather. Mr. Rigsby's wife died many years earlier, and Frank looked for every opportunity to help the elderly gentleman who was now in his mid-eighties. When his lawn needed mowing, Frank tried to anticipate that and take care of it for him. When the many trees around his home shed their mountains of orange, brown, and red leaves each autumn, Frank raked and added them to the gentleman's mulch pile after school or on Saturdays.

Even though Mr. Rigsby ambled slowly around his house, he had been living alone up until now without needing assistance. His mind was sharp, and he was as clear-headed as anyone they knew. Frank and his dad had been with Mr. Rigsby moving some furniture for him the previous day, and he had seemed healthy enough then.

"Okay, son. One of us may call to check on you if we see that we'll be gone longer than we've planned."

"Mr. Whidden, if you don't get an answer here at your house, call *my* house," Griff said. "Frank can eat supper with us tonight."

"Thanks, Griff. We appreciate that. You guys be praying for Mr. Rigsby starting now. We need him to be healthy and stay well for many more years!"

"I won't be away from our house for very long, Dad, in case that soldier from Fort Everett calls."

"I sincerely hope that he does, Frank." Mr. Whidden backed up a few steps and pulled the door closed behind him.

Griff, Frank, and Chase looked at each other in silence until Griff finally spoke.

"That must have been him in the ambulance that passed us earlier when Kate was driving."

"You're probably right about that," Frank agreed. "Okay, let's go back to what we were doing and jot down some notes to figure out what we heard on the tape."

"Well, first, whoever we heard—either they were trespassing, or Mr. Denton let them in," Chase said.

"I'm going to guess that they were trespassing. If you remember, Mr. Denton had to unlock the chain to let us in. That makes me think no one was on the property before we got there. He pushed the gates together but didn't lock them after we went in."

"I agree with you, Chase," Griff said. "And wherever the men said they were going, it was a place where one of them had been before. He said he knew his way around it and he wouldn't need a light?"

"It sounds like whatever they are going to do, it will

31

be after dark. Otherwise, why would the man say he didn't need any sort of light," Frank added.

"What was he talking about when he said '*do-re-mi*'?" Chase asked with a laugh.

"That's just the way some older people used to talk about money," Griff answered. "People sometimes use the word *dough* instead of *money*, and that has to be what he meant."

"Yeah, sometimes you hear old-timers say '*cabbage*,' '*a grand*,' or '*clams*,' or '*Benjamins*' instead of dollars. Those words all mean money," Frank added.

"Okay, so we agree that those two are supposed to deliver something worth a lot of money to someone," Chase said, "but to whom? And what are they selling?"

"Those are the big questions right now," Griff said. "But I'm still not convinced anything illegal is going on. We don't have any proof of that. And to go and tell the Sheriff, my dad would need some solid proof before he could do anything about it."

The grandfather clock in the upstairs hallway chimed four o'clock.

"We won't be eating supper for another two hours. How about we forget about those guys for now and head down to your basement for some games of pool?" Griff began as he stood and addressed Frank. "Then, we can walk over to my house just before 6:00. That way, you won't be away from your house for more than a half-hour in case that soldier calls. Chase, you can eat with us, too, if you want. My mom always makes plenty."

· · · · · · ·

At 6:25, Frank thanked Sheriff and Mrs. Jenkins for the tasty meal, said goodbye to his pals, and walked by himself the half-block to his home. As he turned the key in the back door, he heard the wall phone in the kitchen ringing. He entered the house as fast as he could and picked up the receiver of the telephone.

"Hello."

"Frank, Dad wanted me to check in with you."

"Hi, Kate. Are you still at the hospital in Covington? How is Mr. Rigsby?"

"Yes, we're still here. We've been waiting to learn the results from his brain x-rays."

"Oh, no!" Frank exclaimed. "What happened to him?"

"He fell in his kitchen and hit his head. He was unconscious—they think for about fifteen minutes, or maybe longer. He was finally able to get to his knees, crawl to his phone, and dial the Operator. That's the reason an ambulance came."

"Did he break any bones or anything?"

"I don't think so," Kate replied. "They're going to keep him to observe him for at least a few days. The x-rays they made a half-hour ago were to make sure there wasn't any bleeding in his skull. Once we learn more from the doctors here, we'll be heading home."

"All right, Kate. Everything here is fine. I had supper at Griff's, and I just got home."

"No word from that soldier yet?" Kate asked hopefully.

"Nothing."

"Okay, Frank. I'm praying—we're *all* praying for some good news about Duke. Hopefully, we'll be back to the house in the hour or so."

"Thanks, Kate. Goodbye."

He hung the phone handset back onto its base. Frank walked into the living room and dropped into a stuffed club chair. He reached for the Sunday *Lewisville Ledger* newspaper on the coffee table and thumbed through the news section, followed by the sports section. Frank put it back, unable to care much about anything in its pages. He switched on the television and only halfway watched a weekly variety show. Twenty minutes into the program, the doorbell chimes startled him. Frank glanced through the foyer window and recognized the faded red car parked along the front curb. Even though the sun had nearly set, Frank saw the young blond-haired soldier they'd met at the preserve.

"You found him!" Frank shouted as he stepped onto the porch. Patrick Wilson backed away from the screen door and watched the emotional reunion of a dog and his boy.

"He was pretty far away from the gate," Patrick said, "and he was sniffing around an area with fewer trees than in most parts of the preserve."

"That must have been in the meadow where we last saw him. He ran after a small deer, and when my friends came back without him, I figured—we *all* figured—that Duke was gone for good."

Patrick laughed softly. "Not *forever*, thank goodness. I don't usually hike around that area, but after Kate—your sister, right?"

Frank nodded.

"After your sister told me about Duke, I set out hiking determined I'd find him for you." He chuckled lightly. "And if my voice sounds a little bit hoarse right now, it's because I called Duke's name and hollered for a long time until he finally showed up and came to me."

"Thank you! *Thank you so much, Mr. Wilson,*" Frank announced as he extended his handshake to the soldier.

"It's just Patrick to my friends, Frank. People call my dad Mr. Wilson, but I'm just Patrick to you," he chuckled.

"Okay, Patrick. Can you come in and stay for a few minutes? My parents and sister aren't here, but they should be back in just a little while. I want my mom and dad to meet you. I know they'll want to give you a reward, and we'll pay for your gas..."

The young soldier held up the palm of his hand toward Frank and interrupted him. "No, *no way!* Seeing this fine-looking dog back with his family is the only reward *I* need. But I think *he's* going to need a good brushing and a bath. There were some serious briars where he must have gone. I walked through some muddy and washed-out places in my search, but I think Duke found them all before I did." He laughed as the three of them went into the house, and Frank closed the front door.

"A bath for Duke is *no* problem! He actually *likes* them!"

Frank offered his guest a glass of ice water and gestured with his hand toward the sofa. Patrick sat, Frank returned to the club chair, and Duke laid down next to Frank's feet. After a few seconds, the collie exhaled loudly and rolled onto his side, evidently tired from his adventure.

"So, you go to the preserve to hike—like *a lot*?" Frank asked.

"Yeah, at least I try to," Patrick began. "I've been stationed at Fort Everett for a little over three months—since mid-January—and back in the place where I grew up, we had mountains in all directions from my town. I've always loved the outdoors and still want to hike in the forests as much as possible. Some friends told me about the preserve, so I went one weekend a couple of months ago. I met Mr. Denton, and he said I could come back anytime. It's not that far from my post, so I get to have some of my *thinking* time there whenever I hike."

"I liked being at the preserve today—except, of course, for us losing Duke," Frank said. "It was my first time there since grade school, and I only went today because my sister saw my invention and asked me to help her with her college project."

Patrick's eyes widened. "Your *invention*?"

"Yeah! Let me show it to you. It's on my workbench." Frank stood, and Patrick followed him to the basement. He showed his guest the metal bowl with the microphone attachment.

"Did it work?" the young man asked.

"It did everything I'd hoped it would do!" Frank said with an excited smile. "I recorded all kinds of bird sounds for Kate. And then the strangest thing happened just before Duke ran away. I couldn't see the people, but when I pointed this thing across that clearing, I heard the voices of two men on my headphones. To my friends and me, what they were talking about sounded like they were planning something illegal!"

"That seems like the exact spot where I saw some muddy and washed-out places. Now that I think about it, those might have been rain-filled tire tracks!" Patrick exclaimed.

"But I thought no vehicles were allowed to drive back into the preserve," Frank stated.

They both returned to the steps and began to climb them. "You're right. They're not. It's a rule for everyone who's allowed to go onto the property. Even Mr. Denton can't use his vehicle because they say it disturbs the habitat. They have a small herd of zebras and some antelopes back in there somewhere, along with lots of prized deer. No hunting is ever allowed on the property. There's just one gate, and it's in the front."

Chapter 3

At 7:15, headlights swept across the front windows of the Whidden house, and in another moment, Frank and Patrick heard three car doors open and close. The first person through the back door was Kate, who had recognized the red car parked along the curb. Frank and Patrick rose from their seats and walked toward the arriving sister and parents. Kate's expression became a wide grin when she caught sight of Duke. She squealed his name and leaned over to greet him.

"This is incredible!" Mr. Whidden began. "How did you ever...?" He stopped speaking, extended a handshake to the soldier and hugged Frank. "Thank you, Patrick! But really, we can't ever thank you enough," Frank's dad said. "Kate told us what you said you were willing to try to do."

"It was nothing, sir," Patrick replied. "It was *way* more than luck that I arrived there at the preserve when Kate was leaving. Duke is a great dog, and I can't imagine anyone losing him."

Frank's mother stepped forward. "Thank you *so much*, Patrick! We'd love to reward you for what you've done—at the very *least*, to pay you for your trouble and your gas."

The soldier took a step back. "No, no, that's totally unnecessary. I probably need to be heading back to the base. I'm just really glad everything worked out like it did—after I met your daughter there at the gate." He looked at Kate and nodded toward her.

"Well then, won't you come back again soon when we can feed you a home-cooked meal—maybe for Sunday lunch next weekend?" Mrs. Whidden asked.

"Yes, and before that you could join us at church," Kate added, "unless you have somewhere you need to be on Sunday. But if you can come, after church plan to stay and eat lunch here. We'd love to have you!"

"You don't want to pass on that offer of Mrs. Whidden's cooking, Patrick! And our church is easy to find. It's on your way here," Mr. Whidden explained.

"All right, then, I'd be honored to do those things," Patrick said as he extended his arm, shook Frank's and his dad's hands, and took a step back toward the front door. "I'll see you folks next Sunday morning."

"Just a minute," Frank's dad said. "My office phone number and our home telephone number are on this if you need to contact us." He handed Patrick his business card.

"Ten-thirty at our church. We'll be watching for you!" Kate said.

Patrick rubbed Duke behind the ears, waved goodbye to the four Whiddens, and walked to his car. Frank's father closed the front door and turned to face his family. "If you've ever thought it was useless to pray, I hope that you'll always remember what happened here tonight."

•••••••

Frank squeezed the transmit button on the side of his walkie-talkie. "Breaker, breaker! Griff? Chase? Is

39

anybody on?"

Ten seconds went by, and Griff's voice crackled through the speaker. "*I'm* here, Frank, and you sound especially chipper tonight."

Chase joined the conversation and added his response before Frank could explain. "I agree," he said. "What's going on over there at your house?"

Frank grinned to himself, looked at Duke, and pressed the transmit button. "Someone wants to say hello." He pointed to Duke. "*Woof! Arf! Woof-woof!!*"

"Woohoo!!" Chase laughed and hollered at the same time.

"*I can't believe it!* He came *home!*" Griff exclaimed.

"Yep! It's the best thing that's happened around here all year! The soldier that Kate talked to when we were leaving the preserve came here with Duke around seven o'clock. He just left our house a little while ago. He said that Duke was pretty far into the forest when he found him and that he'd gotten into some briars and some muddy ruts or tire tracks. It seemed almost like I was dreaming when I opened the door and saw my dog on the front porch."

"That is *so* cool!" Griff agreed. "I don't know what I would have done if I had lost my dog."

"I'm so happy for you, Frank," Chase said. "But I'm a little confused. You said he was far from the gate, but he'd gotten mud on him from some tire tracks? I thought Kate told us that no cars or trucks were allowed except on that little gravel driveway we took— just barely inside the main gate."

"That's right! And I also learned tonight that it's the *only* gate into the preserve!" Frank added.

"It didn't seem odd to us at the time, but Chase and I saw what looked like tire tracks when we were back in the woods searching for Duke. Something heavy had rolled over a bunch of little sapling trees and made a path. That much was easy to see!"

Chase broke in, "Okay, guys, let's stop and think about this logically! Frank, we didn't get to write on the list you started. First, you heard the voices of two men saying things that seemed suspicious. Now you say there is only one gate, except Griff and I and that soldier saw tire ruts pretty far into the preserve. I can only think of one explanation for those things." Chase released the transmit button.

"Yeah, I think I know what you're thinking and what might be going on around there," Griff said. "It doesn't sound good to me."

"Let's keep this between the three of us," Frank encouraged. "We need more facts, Griff, before we tell your dad *or* Mr. Rigsby. It could be no big deal, but I'm beginning to doubt that it's as simple as *nothing*, either."

"Okay, because of the teachers' conference day and no classes at school tomorrow, who wants to make a morning bike trip back down to the preserve?" Chase asked. "We can just sorta scout around the outside border of the property and see if anything looks suspicious."

"Count me in!" Frank replied.

"Me, too!" Griff added quickly. "Let's meet at my house after breakfast at 8:30. How does that sound?"

"Bring your walkie-talkies!" Chase suggested. "Goodnight, guys!"

"Remember to pray for Mr. Rigsby," Frank said.

"Will do, Frank!" Griff replied.

• *Monday* •

The sun warmed their faces, but the air was still cool as the boys pedaled the bikes south away from town in the early April morning. They saw only a few cars traveling on the rural road leading to the nature preserve while covering the four-mile trip in single file.

Frank and Griff had strapped on small backpacks that held standard items that any experienced outdoorsman might need. Each had a canteen of fresh water, several sizes of bandages, some chocolate pieces for energy, and a flashlight. Chase wore a belt pack to hold his walkie-talkie, and he carried a few waterproof matches and a small water bottle. None of them knew what the morning might hold, but they were prepared for most situations. All three boys had camped dozens of times and, even at their young ages, were certified in first aid procedures.

"We've reached the back border," Griff announced as they slowed to a stop and straddled their bikes several feet away from the asphalt road. "You can expect to find some chiggers in this grass. It looks like the county hasn't mowed along part of this road for a year."

The twelve-foot-tall chain-link perimeter fence looked impressive behind the weeds, grass, and scrub brush, some of which were nearly as tall as the Bon Air boys. They had stopped their bicycles close to one of the corners of the preserve property. From there, they could see along the fence in two directions. As far as they could observe, the high fence extended into the distance in a perfectly straight and unbroken line. From what Kate had said to Frank, each of the four sides of the property was about a mile in length.

"If there is any break in the fence, *I* can't see it," Frank observed. "How about we split up? You two check along the south fence border on foot, and I'll walk along the west fence. Keep your walkie-talkies on and call me when you get to the end, the next corner."

"Let's lay our bikes down here," Griff suggested as he lowered his in the tall grass. "Nobody passing by will ever see them from the road as high as it is."

For the next fifteen minutes, the team of Chase and Griff pushed and trudged through the overgrown grass along the southern perimeter. The bases of the hundreds of metal fence posts had been set into concrete poured below the ground level, with one post every twelve feet. Stiff loops of metal wire strapped the chain-link material onto each post. This design kept the deer and the exotic animals safe inside from any coyotes or wolves that might try to enter the preserve.

After a while, Frank's voice broke through Griff's radio speaker. "I'm at the end of my length of fence, and I didn't see anything that looked out of order. How about you guys? Over."

Griff unclipped the two-way radio from the front strap of his backpack. "We didn't walk as fast as you, so we have another few hundred yards to get to the corner. But we've seen nothing that looks wrong, either. We'll check back with you in a few more minutes," Griff added. "Over."

"Okay. I'll keep going around the corner and start

to walk along the northern property line," Frank said. "Whenever you call, I'll turn around and head back to where we started. And, by the way, this part along the fence *has* been recently mowed. Over and out."

"Ten-four, Frank. Over and out," Griff replied.

Three minutes later, Griff's voice blasted through Frank's radio speaker. His tone seemed urgent.

"Frank, we've made it to the corner, and it looks like we stumbled onto something—something that shouldn't be here!"

Frank immediately turned around and doubled the speed of his steps. *What is it, Griff?*

"It looks like somebody has used a bolt cutter and clipped the chain-link fence from the bottom to around eight or nine feet high. There are two long cuts eleven or twelve feet apart close to each fence post. There are also a couple of ropes hanging down where the cuts are—one on either side. It's hard to describe what we're seeing, but someone could pull on the ropes and roll up that cut section of the fence. The cuts are up high enough that a car or a pick-up truck could get into the preserve through this opening. It's hidden really well. If you weren't looking for it, you'd never notice it. Get here as fast as you can! You need to see this."

By this time, Frank was jogging and breathing hard. *"I'm on my way. Stay put."*

Less than ten minutes later, Frank had run more than a mile along the fence and was sweating when he reached Chase and Griff. Griff offered his canteen to Frank. "You need to drink some water before you do anything else."

Frank willingly drank from it while Chase pointed

out where the fence metal was clipped. "Since someone cut this section between the posts and only clipped it partway from the bottom, you can hardly notice it. If the grass and weeds between the fence and the road were cut low like they are along the other sides of the preserve," he said while pointing to the growth, "it would be a whole lot easier to see. These trees inside the fence hang over a lot of the fence line so that they shade the area right here."

Griff added, "If you wanted the ideal place to break into the preserve and hide your gate, this is it."

Frank stepped back and noticed how well the opening was made. He looked in both directions along the road and then pointed. "Except for that abandoned house across the road—that one where the tree branch has broken through the roof, the two on either side of it are pretty far away," Frank noted. "Someone could pull a vehicle off the road along here and stay next to the fence until they reached this gate, and the tall grass would even hide their tire tracks. It's *perfect*."

"Should we lift the cut fence and go in?" Chase asked while looking at Frank.

"As much as I'd like to do that, I think we'd better not—not without Mr. Rigsby's permission, anyway. Let's head back to our neighborhood and think about what our next move ought to be."

"I have an idea of what we *can* do," Chase said excitedly. "I'll show you what I'm thinking when we get to my house."

"Sounds great!" both boys replied.

• • • • • • •

45

At the Spencers' house, Frank and Griff followed Chase to the second-floor hallway outside of his bedroom door. Chase pulled on a short rope above their heads. It was attached to a set of pull-down steps that led to the attic.

"I'll need a minute to find something. You can go on into my room, and I'll be there soon," Chase suggested.

Through the ceiling above the bedroom, Frank and Griff heard the sounds of thumping, scraping, and footsteps as Chase dragged boxes around in his search. In another moment, they heard him climb down the folding stairs, push them up, and close the opening.

"Got it!" Chase announced as he entered his bedroom. He was holding a simple black plastic device shaped like a cube. "It's a Brownie Six-20." Chase began to open the small camera, and he placed it on his desk. "Here's what I'm thinking: we can strap this down to a board. With a little metal eyelet pushed into the wood, we can attach some clear fishing line to the camera's shutter button. Then we can stretch out that line through the eyelet and attach the other end to the bottom of that chain-link fence—the part that rolls up. When someone comes along to lift the fence and go into the preserve, doing that will yank the fishing line, pull on the shutter button, and snap a photograph. If we put the camera on the ground in the grass next to the fence, I don't think anyone will ever notice it."

"And then *I* can develop the film in the darkroom in my basement!" Griff added excitedly. "It's a *great* plan, and it's the best thing we can do for now since we can't hang out there indefinitely and watch for someone to show up. But maybe this way, we can figure out who is trespassing!"

"Let's do it, guys!" Frank said. "Do you have the board? And the fishing line?"

"I do," Chase answered. "We have everything we'll need. Come on out to the garage with me!"

. . . .

After cutting a 12-inch by 12-inch piece of three-quarter-inch thick plywood, Chase handed the board to Frank. Frank drilled a hole near each of the four corners. He also drilled two more holes a bit farther apart than the width of the camera through which to run a wire. Griff took the wood behind the garage and sprayed it with some dark green paint that Chase had found on a shelf. Frank noticed a croquet set with balls, mallets, and wickets stored in the garage. Chase said they could borrow four croquet wickets and slide one side of the wicket wire into each of the four corners. He believed that when they pushed those four wires into the ground, the board with the camera attached to it would stay in place even if a big gust of wind came along. Chase tossed a spool of fishing line to Frank, who stuffed it into his backpack. Chase then loaded a roll of fresh film into the camera, wedged the board under the luggage carrier above his bicycle's rear fender, and the three of them headed down the driveway and into the street.

"It looks like no rain is expected for the next few days, so we should be good to go!" Griff commented as they pedaled their bikes to the end of the block.

"Hey, here comes Donnie!" Frank said. They all

heard the low rumble of his car's glass pack mufflers.

Donnie was Chase's college-aged cousin and one of the Bon Air boys' best friends. From the time he turned fourteen years old, Donnie had delivered *Lewisville Ledger* newspapers from his bicycle to a quarter of the town's homes. For the following two years, he had saved most of his money. Then on his sixteenth birthday, once he got his driver's license, Donnie spent most of his savings and bought a used Chevy Bel Air coupe. While he continued to deliver papers, Donnie held on to birthday money and his weekly earnings and used it to repair and restore the coupe. He put white tuck-and-roll vinyl on the seats and door panels. Donnie painted the car with royal blue metal flake paint and added moondisc wheel covers. Finally, he installed glass pack mufflers. Frank, Griff, and Chase were sure that it was the coolest car in all of Jeffers County.

Donnie slowed and came alongside the three boys on their bicycles, then he reached across the passenger seat and cranked the curbside window down.

"Enjoying your day out of school, I see," he chuckled and then said, "Where are you guys headed?"

Chase stopped, straddled the bicycle's frame, and walked his bike closer to Donnie's window. "It's kind of a long story, but we are headed to the nature preserve. We're on a mission and need to hide a camera."

"Another mystery, huh?" Donnie said with a wink. "I can save you three some time and effort if you want to park your bikes and let me drive you there. I have some free time."

"We won't turn that offer down!" Griff said. "Give us a minute to go back to Chase's and leave them."

The three boys turned around and pedaled the short distance to Chase's driveway while Donnie backed up and waited on the street for them.

Frank and Griff crawled into the coupe's back seat, and Chase slid into the front passenger seat of his cousin's car. He held the painted board, wire wickets, and spool of fishing line on his lap. Griff kept the camera.

"So, what is this mission about, if you don't mind me asking?" Donnie inquired, looking over at Chase.

"Yesterday, we spent a little time with Kate at the nature preserve. Frank lost his dog there..."

"DUKE! You lost *Duke*?" Donnie interrupted as he looked at Frank in his rearview mirror.

"Only for a few hours," Frank said and then smiled. "He's back home again, thanks to a soldier who was hiking on the property."

Chase spoke again. "Frank built this cool parabolic reflector microphone thing and was recording bird calls for a project Kate is doing for college. He couldn't see anyone, but he heard some men's voices over his headphones. They said some things that seemed pretty suspicious, and we think they were probably trespassing."

Griff added to the explanation and said, "So we went back to the property this morning and walked along the perimeter of the fence. It looks to us like someone has cut into the back border fence and made an opening big enough for a car or truck."

Donnie whistled softly. "That's *very* strange! Have you told Mr. Rigsby about any of this? You realize, don't you, that he owns all of that property?"

"I learned that yesterday from my dad," Frank replied. "But Mr. Rigsby is in the hospital now after he fell and hit his head at his home yesterday."

"I didn't realize that. Will he be okay?"

"We *think* he will be," Frank replied. "My parents and Kate went to see him last night."

"Okay, now that I'm all caught up, what's your plan today?" Donnie asked.

"We are going to hide a camera about ten feet from the fence opening—close to where someone cut into it," Frank answered. "We'll run a tripwire from the fence to the shutter button on the camera."

Chase continued the explanation from the front seat. "Whoever lifts the chain-link fence to get into the back part of the preserve will take a picture of himself!"

Griff spoke next. "We don't have any real evidence of anything wrong happening there except that, according to the caretaker, no vehicles are allowed inside the preserve. We saw what looked like tire tracks pretty far into the forest. And there is only supposed to be one gate—the one by Mr. Denton's little house."

•••••••

When they arrived at the perimeter road behind the preserve, Chase directed Donnie to where the boys found the cuts in the fence—at the hidden entrance. Donnie parked on the shoulder of the road, and they all walked to the place that Chase felt would be the best spot to hide the camera.

The combined heights of the mounting board and camera were around eight inches. So when they were placed on the ground in five-foot-tall grass, the boys were sure nobody would notice them. Griff removed some of the thickest grass from directly in front of the camera so the lens would have an opening to get a clear photo of any intruder. Frank tilted the front of the board up a little by wedging some small rocks under its edge. They anchored the corners with the four croquet wicket wires pushed through the holes and into the ground. Donnie and Chase attached the fishing line onto the bottom corner of the chain-link gate. Since they used transparent fishing line, it was almost invisible, even to them. They rolled out more of the line back to the camera, stretched it tightly, and tied the end to the camera's shutter button.

"If anyone goes into the preserve here between those two fence posts, we'll get a photograph of him," Frank said as he admired their setup.

"You guys amaze me!" Donnie said as they returned to the car, and he patted his cousin Chase on his shoulder. "I hope you'll let me know whatever you find out."

"Oh, we *will*, Donnie! I can promise you that," Griff said with a smile.

Chapter 4

Two days later, on Wednesday, between their first and second classes, the Bon Air boys met in their school's hallway next to Frank's locker.

"I'm about to go crazy thinking about that camera we hid!" Chase said with a look of pretended concern.

"Well, buddy, we don't want to be responsible for you losing your mind, so tell me, when do you guys think we oughta go to check on it?" Griff asked.

"Well, *I* believe we should head there right after school today," Chase answered. "The weather report this morning on the radio said there is a fifty percent chance of rain tonight. My camera isn't waterproof, so I'm ready to go back and get it."

"Yeah," Frank agreed, "and we're halfway to the preserve if we leave from here at school. If anyone has tripped the shutter button, we will see that right away."

The warning bell announcing the next class period rang in the hall just as Frank spoke. "Either way, photo or not, we need to collect Chase's camera." He then turned to Griff. "If it *did* snap a photo, will you have time later tonight to develop the film and make a print of it?"

"No problem, amigo!" The three of them walked together toward their classroom. "If anybody has been there and rolled up the gate, I ought to have a photo to show you guys by suppertime!"

·······

The rest of the morning seemed to the boys like it happened in slow motion. When the friends came together in the cafeteria at lunchtime, Griff, Frank, and Chase sat in a corner away from the other students. Between bites of peanut butter sandwiches, potato chips, apples, and gulps from their five-cent cartons of milk, they exchanged their thoughts about what might be happening at the back fence line of the preserve.

Once the dismissal bell rang at 3:00, they were the first to reach the bicycle rack. In less than ten minutes, they had covered the distance to the place along the perimeter where they'd hidden the camera. Their hearts were racing as they laid down their bikes on the grass. Chase ran ahead and was the first to reach the hidden chain-link gate.

"Someone's been here!" he shouted.

Griff went directly to the camera, also, and knelt beside it. "Oh yeah! The fishing line has been pulled. The hook isn't attached to the chain-link anymore, and it definitely snapped the shutter. Somebody has opened this gate!"

"We can't know exactly *when* it happened, and that isn't important right now," Frank stated. "What matters is that *just maybe* the camera caught a person's face in the photo."

The boys rolled up the fishing line, and Chase stowed it and the camera in his backpack. They left behind the wooden platform they had anchored in the ground with the four wickets. The boys agreed that they might return later with the camera and get another photo once the rain had come and gone.

When they had reached the town limits and passed

53

their school while heading home, Chase began to lag behind his friends. It became much more difficult for him to pedal and keep up with them. When he glanced down, he realized why.

"Guys, my back tire is almost flat! We need to go by the filling station so I can put some air in it."

"All right, Chase, we'll slow down. The closest place with an air pump isn't very far away," Griff said.

Marvin's Fill-Up, a combination gas station and mini-grocery, was directly across the road from the Lewisville Lodge. When the boys arrived, they noticed that a car and a truck were parked on either side of the pump island. Marvin Hobson, dressed in stained light-blue coveralls and sporting a faded orange ball cap with a big grease spot on the turned-up brim, moved between the truck and car. The chest pocket of his coveralls was partly torn away on one side, and the three ballpoint pens and tire pressure gauge clipped onto it were dangerously close to falling out. He carried a red rag in one of his hands to remove radiator caps and check oil levels.

The air dispenser at Marvin's Fill-Up was mounted on the same island as the two gas pumps and was centered between them. The gasoline nozzle from one pump was pushed into the filler opening of the truck, but the driver was nowhere in sight. The pump had cut off by itself before the boys had arrived.

"It looks like one of those two people will have to move before we can get to the air dispenser," Griff noted. "While we're waiting, let's go into the store, and I'll buy everybody a bottle of root beer."

Frank made a silent *"Wow!"* with his mouth and

then poked a finger into Griff's ribs. "Mr. Big Spender here doesn't show up every day, so let's grab his offer while we can, Chase!" They all laughed, went inside, and pulled three bottles from the cooler. After they pried the caps from the bottles, Griff paid the clerk, and they walked outdoors and waited while Marvin finished washing the car's windows. After checking the oil, he closed the hood and collected for the gas purchase. Then the driver pulled away.

Chase rolled his bike to the island where the car had just been, dialed 40 pounds of pressure into the air pump, and began to fill the bike tire. When he had finished and the boys were preparing to leave, they noticed a man walk out of the store and get behind the wheel of the truck. Marvin pulled a receipt book from his shirt pocket and stepped to the driver's window. The person in the truck signed the receipt, started his engine, and drove away from the filling station.

The boys mounted their bikes and headed for their neighborhood in the opposite direction.

"I have an extra inner tube at my house for your tire if you need one, Chase," Frank said.

"I'll let you know if it loses any air between now and after supper. Thanks for the offer," Chase said.

"And later tonight, I'll call you both on your walkie-talkies after I develop and print the film," Griff told the two.

At the end of the Jenkins' driveway, Chase handed the camera to Griff.

"I hope something interesting got captured on that film," Frank said.

. . . .

With an hour remaining until suppertime and very little homework assigned for the night, Griff dropped his backpack on his bedroom floor. While holding Chase's Brownie camera, he bounded down the stairs and stepped into the kitchen to find his mother, Barbara Jenkins, standing at the sink peeling potatoes.

"Do you need my help with anything, Mom?" Griff asked.

"Everything here seems to be under control, son," she said. "Thanks for the offer though."

"Then I'm going to be downstairs in the darkroom for a little while."

"All right. I'll call you and Geoff to the supper table when your dad gets home."

The back door swung open. "Did I hear someone mention my name?" a grinning eight-grader said from the rear porch entry.

Geoff Jenkins was Griff's brother, a year younger and an inch shorter, but ten pounds heavier than Griff. He was a standout athlete at school on three different Lewisville Lions sports teams.

Barbara Jenkins turned to her second son, "Griff is about to work with a camera or film or something, and I told him I would call you both to supper within the hour."

"Oh, can I *please* watch?" Geoff asked eagerly, showing Griff a goofy grin. He closed the back door and hurried to join his brother.

"You can come and watch, Geoff, *IF* you promise you won't get scared and start crying when I have to turn off the lights," Griff said as he reached for the doorknob and winked toward their mother. "You *do* realize that our darkroom is *dark* inside!"

Geoff dropped his gym bag and backpack on the living room floor, then rushed to Griff from behind, wrapping his brother with a friendly bear hug. *"You're my hero!"* Geoff said with a silly voice and another corny smile. "I know *you'll* protect me!"

Griff rolled his eyes, shook his head, and led the way down the steps.

Their dad was a hobby photographer and had built a small darkroom in the corner of the Jenkins' basement. In that space, he had added a countertop that held a sink with available hot and cold water. Stretched above the counter was a length of twine with a dozen wooden clothespins clipped to it so Griff could hang film negatives or photo papers as they dried. The brothers stepped into the room, and Griff closed and locked the door behind them.

"So what's on the film, and whose camera is that?" Geoff asked.

"We honestly aren't sure about the film," Griff replied, "and the camera belongs to Chase." He wasn't ready to explain the Bon Air boys' discovery to anyone else just yet. "It's an experiment that the guys and I set up. It might not be anything, but I need to take a look."

Griff carefully removed the film from the camera using a dark bag and threaded it into a lightproof canister. Over the following minutes, he added and removed different chemical baths to develop the exposed image on the film strip.

"We're about to learn what Chase's little camera saw," Griff said to Geoff. He removed and washed then lightly dried the strip and held the only frame with an image on it up to the overhead light. Satisfied that the negative looked correctly exposed, he used his scissors and cut a six-inch piece from the full negative strip. "Let's put this in the enlarger and make a print."

Griff switched the photo enlarger on and fed the film into its slot. He lightly pulled on the negative, lining up the image being projected onto the white surface below.

Geoff cocked his head to one side, then to the other as he studied the projected image. "What am I looking at?"

"Remember that this is a negative, so everything that our eyes would normally see as white or light will look black or a shade of gray here. And everything that looks black or dark to our eyes is white or gray here. It'll be easier to figure it all out when I print it on a sheet of photo paper."

Griff arranged three trays and poured into each of them a half inch of one of three different, special chemicals.

At this point, only the red-tinted safety light bulb illuminated the darkroom. Griff opened a flat box and removed an 8-inch by 10-inch piece of photographic paper. He placed it on the enlarger bed, where he had projected the negative image.

"Now, let's try six seconds of light exposure onto the paper for this one," Griff suggested to himself.

He turned on the enlarger and eyed his wristwatch as the second hand swept that brief time. Griff immediately switched off the enlarger, picked up the paper with small tongs, and laid it into the fluid of the first tray. His heart raced as he watched the paper gradually turn from white into grays and blacks and soon become an actual image!

"All of this makes sense now," Geoff said, as Griff used the tongs again, moved the paper to the middle tray, and then finally into the last one. He let the excess fluid from the photo paper drip into the sink. Then he lifted the new print to the overhead twine and attached it at eye level with two clothespin clips.

"Turn on the lights, please, brother," Griff requested. "Let's see what we have here."

In the photo, the two boys saw the rear half of a truck. Also visible, standing in front of the truck and seen from the waist down, was a man wearing work boots and dungarees! It was the first real evidence— just what the Bon Air boys needed to begin to build their case.

"Is that what you were expecting?" Geoff asked, revealing a confused expression.

"It's a start!" Griff said.

"See those toolboxes along the side of the truck?" Geoff remarked as he pointed to the photo. "That looks like the kind of truck someone uses who does outdoor work or construction things."

"That's a great observation, and I feel as though I've seen one like that somewhere around town recently," Griff added.

Through the closed door of the darkroom, they heard from the top of the stairs, *"Boys, your dad is home. It's time to eat!"*

Griff turned to his brother. "This photo is part of an experiment, so, for now, let's keep this between you and me—okay?"

"I *love* a good mystery," Geoff said, displaying an ear-to-ear smile. *"Sure!"*

•••••••

After their suppers, the three Bon Air boys wrapped up school assignments, then they headed for their bedrooms and switched on walkie-talkies.

Frank called the other two at eight o'clock, and after they both replied, he spoke first. "My dad was late getting home, so we just now finished eating. He came straight from the hospital after visiting Mr. Rigsby. He's doing better, but is sometimes still a little dizzy from hitting his head, so the doctors want him to stay until the weekend."

"I'm glad they believe that Mr. Rigsby will get to go home fairly soon," Chase commented. "By Saturday, he will have been there almost a week."

Frank agreed with Chase and then changed the tone of his voice to a playful one. "And Griff, do you have anything you want to tell us—anything about a certain *photograph?*"

"I *do*," Griff began. "I developed and printed the film when I got home." He released the walkie-talkie button, stopped transmitting, and left his statement hanging unfinished in the air. Griff smiled to himself, knowing that his friends were eager to learn what was on the film.

After fifteen seconds of silence, Chase spoke. "I guess you're going to make us come over to your house and see the picture for ourselves, right?"

Griff chucked into his radio. "You can come if you want, but in the meantime, I'll describe it to you." He stopped transmitting and reached for the photo.

"Wait!" Frank shouted into his radio. "Earlier this afternoon, Mr. Rigsby told my dad that he would like for Kate to bring him a couple of books from his nightstand—ones he's been reading. I volunteered to go and get them tonight since we have a spare key to his house. How about if you guys meet me at the curb by my driveway in ten minutes, and we'll walk there together? Griff, bring the photo with you and that way we can all see it. Okay?"

The others agreed, and they each switched off their radio.

·······

At 8:15, the three friends began the five-minute walk to Goldstone Lane and Mr. Rigsby's house. Griff carried a manilla envelope containing the printed photo, and he planned to unveil it for Frank and Chase inside the gentleman's home in the light of the foyer.

As they were almost at the house, Griff abruptly froze. He quickly raised his hand, signaling Frank and Chase to stop.

"Look!" Griff whispered as he pointed ahead.

"What? Oh, *wow*!" Chase was the next to see it.

"That's not supposed to be happening!" Frank exclaimed.

A light flickered from inside a window on the third floor. It grew bright and then darker, and each of the boys instantly realized that someone was in Mr. Rigsby's attic. As that person moved the light around in random directions, it sometimes shined on the window that faced the street.

"What should we do?" Chase whispered.

"Let me think for a minute," Griff said quietly as he led the other two boys closer to the large house. "How about this—you guys go across the street and get behind the bushes. Stand where you can still see the house and watch that window. I'll sneak onto the front porch, ring the doorbell, and run back to you. We can watch what happens. Maybe that person will leave when I do that and show himself."

"That sounds like a good plan—a pretty safe one!" Frank agreed.

In the pale yellow light of an almost-full moon, Chase and Frank got into position on the far side of Goldstone Lane. Griff slipped the photo envelope under his jacket. Then out of view of anyone inside the house, he pressed himself against the trunk of a large tree near the curb. When he was sure that the path was clear, he moved slowly and silently toward the Rigsby house. Griff reached the porch, tiptoed up the front steps, rang the doorbell, and dashed across the street into the shadows next to his friends.

Immediately after Griff rang the bell, Frank and Chase saw the light in the attic window go dark. Only the sounds of a few crickets broke the stillness of the night. No cars passed the house or went by them in either direction. A minute passed—then two. In the distance—they guessed a half-block away—a dog barked two times, and then everything became quiet again. Suddenly, they heard a car door close from somewhere not far away, followed by the sound of a motor starting. They couldn't see a vehicle or any headlights from their position, but several seconds later, a motor revved and a vehicle drove away. Soon, the motor sounds faded, and the night was quiet again.

"I guess that's that," Frank observed. "They must have been parked behind the house and then left by the back door."

"That'd be my guess, too," Chase added.

"Let's not assume that whoever was in the attic has left the house," Griff cautioned. "We need to get closer and then go around to the back to see if anything might be going on at the rear of the place. Follow me, guys. Stay close, but be ready to run if we find somebody back there," Griff directed.

They crossed the road in single file and headed for the west side of the house. Being careful to step carefully and lightly, Griff led them to the rear corner, where the boys stopped and regrouped. From there, they had a clear view of the backyard with its many trees, the large back porch, and the carriage house that served as Mr. Rigsby's garage. The moonlight shined brightly on all of that area, but they saw no vehicle or people anywhere.

"This sure is strange," Frank whispered. "Let's check and see if anything looks like it's been messed with on the porch or around the back door."

Chase pulled a penlight from his pocket and shined it around on the grass. As they moved from the corner of the house to the porch, he suddenly stopped.

"Hold up, guys! Look!"

Chase pointed to the grass along the bottom of a tall wooden trellis covered in vines of ivy. The painted trellis had openings made of thin boards that formed the shapes of diamonds. It started at the ground and went up the side of the house to the eave. The flashlight revealed many ivy leaves torn from the vines and lying on the grass. Chase stepped back from the house and shined his light up the full height of the trellis. All of the boys followed the beam upward and then gasped at what they saw. It was evident that someone had recently climbed up the trellis breaking off many ivy leaves as they did. Several of the thin trellis boards were cracked or loosened. *A third-floor window into the attic stood wide open above the eave at the top of the house!*

Chapter 5

"So *that's* how he got into the attic!" Frank exclaimed.

"It sure looks that way. But it might be more than just a *he*. It could be a *they*," Griff added. "We don't know how many people were up there."

"Or if they are *still* inside!" Chase added as he pointed toward the top floor. He again trained his flashlight beam onto the yard around the base of the trellis. Reflections of his light sparkled in the grass. "Look, guys! There's broken glass here, and I'll bet it came from the window up there."

"I think we need to go inside and look around," Frank said.

The others shot surprised glances at him.

Frank continued, "After all, we came here to get some books. We need to do that, plus we ought to see if anything has been disturbed or taken." He turned to his friends. "It's okay if you don't want to go in with me. I'll go by myself."

"*No*, Frank! You're *not* going in there alone," Griff said indignantly.

"Will your key open the back door?" Chase asked.

"I think so," Frank answered. "Let's find out."

They climbed the porch steps, and Chase shined his light on the door's deadbolt lock while Frank inserted and turned the key then turned the doorknob.

"Chase," Griff began, "why don't you stay here on the porch and keep an eye out for anybody or anything in the backyard that doesn't belong there. Just yell into the house if you need us. And I'd like to borrow your penlight so we won't have to turn on any lamps when we're inside."

Griff led Frank into the house while Chase settled back against the doorframe. All of the boys, especially Frank, had been in the house enough times to know right away that nothing downstairs seemed out of place. They approached the front foyer where the wide staircase rose, turned, rose even higher, and turned again. Some of the oak steps creaked and popped loudly under their weight. The shadows made by the flashlight along the walls created weird shapes as the boys ascended the stairs and reached the second floor.

"Mr. Rigsby's bedroom is down this hallway," Frank said in a quieter-than-normal voice as he pointed to their left.

Griff walked ahead of Frank holding the penlight that illuminated their path into the room. The furnishings in Mr. Rigsby's bedroom were made from dark mahogany wood. The bed's four corner posts appeared to be almost as thick as telephone poles, and they were taller than either boy could reach. An oversized chair faced the bed. It had a padded seat and back covered with dark green velvet, and its carved wooden armrests gave the chair the appearance of a throne. An antique wardrobe with double doors and heavy brass handles filled most of the wall alongside the door. A large fireplace and hearth were located on the wall facing the foot of the bed.

"This place is *amazing*! It's almost like a palace!" Griff said reverently.

Frank walked toward the head of the bed and stopped at a nightstand that held a candlestick lamp draped with hanging crystal prisms around its edge. On the table was a biography of Winston Churchill and a Bible, and he gathered both of them in his hands.

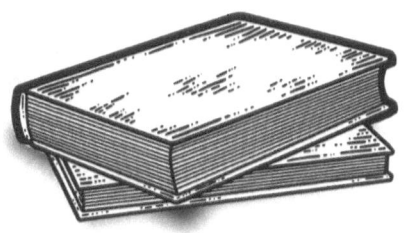

"I guess that's all we can do here," Frank said.

"I'd like to take a quick look in the attic," Griff said as they returned to the second-floor hall.

Frank swallowed hard. "Okay—if you think that's safe. The steps that lead up to it are down there—at the far end," he said, pointing past the main staircase. Griff led the way, and Frank slowed and stooped just long enough to place the two books on the floor by the top step. They continued ahead and paused at the attic door. Griff turned the knob, and suddenly *the door swung open and hit him in the chest!* A shadowy figure burst into the hallway ramming Griff with his shoulder. The intruder spun him around and knocked the flashlight from his hand. Frank, too surprised to react, fell backward as the man pushed him into a wall with one hand and then thundered past him to the stairs. The man stumbled over the two books, lost his balance, and fell forward. He twisted his ankle when he missed the first step and slid on his backside down the flight of stairs to the point where they turned. The man groaned in pain and then rose to his feet.

"CHASE!" Griff yelled to his friend at the back door using all of the air in his lungs. *"WATCH OUT! SOMEBODY'S IN HERE!"*

On the remaining steps, the large man moved much more slowly. He dragged his right leg and hopped the rest of the way, putting his weight on his left foot.

Both Frank and Griff moved to the rail and watched the back of the dark figure from above as he struggled to turn the front door lock and knob. He finally yanked it open and lumbered into the night.

Griff started down the steps as Chase eased into their view below the rail. Frank strained to see into the darkness of the second-floor landing and looked in both directions, fearing that another intruder might still show up. He gathered the books from the floor and hurriedly caught up with his friend soon after Griff reached the bottom step.

In an instant, fear had pushed adrenaline into the bloodstreams of the three boys. Because of the scary incident on the second floor, they each trembled as if they were suddenly thrust into freezing weather.

"What just happened?" Chase asked, his voice barely producing any sound.

"Whoever climbed up the trellis didn't leave that way. He must have heard us talking when we were in the backyard," Griff imagined.

"*Or* when we came up the stairs," Frank added. "I guess he was expecting to make his escape through the front door, but then *we* showed up."

"I had a profile view of the guy when he was trying to get the door open," Chase explained. "It didn't seem like he took anything—at least he wasn't holding anything that I could see. What do you think he was doing in here?"

"That's what we need to find out," Griff insisted, "but not tonight. Whoever he is, he's going to be limping for a while and probably not climbing another trellis anytime soon. I think we're through here for now. We have those books, so let's just go home."

"Kate is supposed to take me to Mr. Rigsby's hospital room after school tomorrow," Frank said. "He needs to know about the break-in, and maybe he can tell me what valuable thing someone would have been looking for in the attic."

"I'd like to go," Chase said.

"Me, too," Griff added, "and I also think it's time for me to tell my dad about some of the things we've learned."

Both of the others nodded in agreement. Frank closed and locked the front door from the inside, and Chase led them through the dark house. From the porch, Frank used the key to lock the back door deadbolt. Now on the outside, the three friends stepped into the yard, where they stood for a moment and talked about how thankful they were none of them had been hurt during the intruder's exit.

Griff removed the envelope from his waistband and slid the photo enlargement into the moonlight. Chase shined his flashlight on it.

"There's no way to identify this guy, but you can see what your camera captured," Griff said. "And I think

I've seen that truck before."

Chase and Frank examined it and commented on how clear it was. With only a few distant crickets breaking the silence of the moonlit night, the Bon Air boys looked into the trees beyond the carriage house, glanced up at the broken window, and began walking to their homes.

·······

• *Thursday* •

Griff rushed into the kitchen with his mop of brown hair uncombed and half of his front shirttail untucked.

"Is Dad still here?" he asked anxiously.

"Good morning, son," Barbara Jenkins said as she looked over her shoulder from the stove. She was tending a skillet lined with sizzling strips of bacon. "Your dad had an early meeting with the mayor and some of the county commissioners."

His brother Geoff was seated at the kitchen table, waiting for the breakfast of eggs, bacon, and biscuits with apple butter. He looked up at Griff from behind his opened history textbook. "You missed him last night, too. You should stay home more," Geoff chided with a half-smile and then lowered his eyes to the book's pages.

"And you should study at night, little brother, so you wouldn't need to cram for a test right before classes," Griff said with a satisfied grin. He dropped his backpack onto the floor and stuffed the remainder of his shirttail into his jeans.

"Boys, be nice to each other," their mother remarked while trying to hide her smile. She knew her sons well and that this was their usual way of lovingly saying "*Good morning!*" or "*I think you are a pretty cool brother.*"

"Your dad had a very long day at work yesterday, and knowing that he had to leave before sunrise today, he went on to bed when he got home last night. Is there anything I can do for you, son?" she asked Griff.

"No, thanks, Mom. I'll just catch up with Dad at suppertime tonight."

Geoff caught his older brother's attention and winked one eye in an exaggerated motion. He supposed that Griff's eager interest in talking to their Sheriff father had something to do with the photograph they'd both seen in the darkroom the afternoon before.

"Frank said that Chase and I could go with him and Kate after school to see Mr. Rigsby," Griff mentioned as he helped his mother place their breakfast food on the table. He pulled back her chair and seated her.

"That would be very good of you boys to have that visit. He is such a nice person," she remarked. "I was very sorry to learn of his fall. Some of the ladies at church have found an adjustable bed to put into his formal dining room for the next few weeks. One of them learned that his doctor didn't want Mr. Rigsby to go up or down the stairs for a while once he returned home. If he became dizzy while on the steps, it could be extremely dangerous for him. Some other ladies are lining up meals to leave for him until he can take care of himself again."

After their meal, both brothers offered to clear the

table and rinse the dishes, but Mrs. Jenkins insisted that they leave them in place. She stepped behind Griff and pulled her fingers through her oldest son's wavy hair, trying to put it at least somewhat in order. In another moment, the brothers grabbed their book bags, dashed out the door, and mounted their bicycles.

When they reached the end of the driveway, Geoff spoke. "I wasn't going to spill your photograph news until you're ready to tell Dad, but I wish you'd tell *me* what's up. Where did you go last night?" Geoff asked as they turned their bikes onto Stafford Avenue.

"It was pretty crazy," Griff began. "Frank, Chase, and I walked over to Mr. Rigsby's house around 8:15. Frank was going over there anyway to get some books that were up in the bedroom. They both wanted to see the photo you and I printed, and I planned to show it to them while the three of us were there together."

"What was so crazy about *that*?" Geoff inquired.

Griff hesitated and then stopped his bicycle. Geoff stopped his as well. "You *still* can't mention this to anyone, but a man was in Mr. Rigsby's house—in the attic. We thought he had gone, but we kinda ran into him when we were upstairs in the hall and he was coming down from the third floor."

"*Whew!*" Geoff whistled aloud. "This sounds like it's getting serious, Griff. Be careful, okay? You'll *have* to tell Dad about that now. And, if you ever need some extra muscle to back you up, I'm always available to go with you three."

Griff reached out and punched Geoff's shirtsleeve over his upper arm. "I will keep that in mind, big guy!" Griff said with a grin, and then he rolled his eyes.

·······

At the end of the school day, the Bon Air boys met again at the school's rear entrance by the bicycle rack.

"Kate will be waiting for us at my house when we get there," Frank said as the three friends began to pedal away from the parking lot.

"That's good. But man, oh man, was this ever a packed day!" Griff said. "I hardly saw either of you except in the hallway between classes."

"I felt that way too," Chase agreed. "And I've been thinking a lot about how we'll need to gently let Mr. Rigsby know what happened at his house last night. I don't want the news to upset him."

"Yeah," Frank began, "but let's decide about that *after* we see how he's feeling. It may be that we shouldn't mention it at all today—or at least for now."

"I agree," Griff added, "and, by the way, I didn't have the chance *again* to tell my dad about the man in the attic or anything else about this mystery. He was already asleep when I got home, and he went into town for an early meeting by the time I got downstairs for breakfast."

"Maybe more pieces of this crazy puzzle will come together after we visit with Mr. Rigsby today, and then you can fill your dad in with some of the details afterward. Let's hope so, anyway," Chase said.

·······

As they rode their bikes into the Whiddens' driveway and parked them near the garage, Kate stepped onto the back porch carrying the two books and pulled the door closed behind her.

"Is everybody ready?" she asked.

"Definitely!" Chase replied.

As they climbed into the car, Griff and Chase took their seats behind Frank and his sister.

"Dad heard from Patrick Wilson by telephone this afternoon at his office," Kate began as she backed the car from the driveway onto the street. "Patrick learned this morning that he has guard duty starting on Saturday night at ten o'clock, so he asked if he could come to spend the day on Saturday. He hoped that would be okay because he didn't want to miss the home-cooked meal mom had offered."

"They said it would be all right, didn't they?" Frank asked excitedly.

"That looks like the plan at this point," Kate replied.

From the back seat, Griff asked, "Is he the fellow who found your dog?"

"Yeah, he's a great guy!" Frank turned and answered. "Patrick comes in town and hikes the trails in the preserve when he gets a weekend pass and can leave Fort Everett. You'll have a chance to meet him if you come over on Saturday afternoon. We invited him to have a meal with us as a way of saying thanks for finding Duke."

•••••••

The Covington Community Hospital was a simple, one-story brick building that had rooms for thirty-four beds. Kate found a parking spot for their sedan only a few spaces from the front entrance. The boys got out of the car feeling anxious, and all of them hoping to find their elderly friend in good spirits and with his health improving. Frank carried Mr. Rigsby's Bible and the biography from the bedroom nightstand. The four of them entered the building through the automatic doors, and they stopped at the reception desk to pick up their visitor badges. The small waiting room smelled like antiseptic and freshly waxed floor tiles. Once they had signed in, they followed Kate down a hallway to the barely opened door of his room.

The curtains over the window were closed, and it seemed to them in the half-darkness that Mr. Rigsby was dozing. The kindly man looked smaller than usual in his hospital bed. Kate knocked very softly and spoke his name. He turned his head toward them and opened his gray-blue eyes. A smile immediately filled his face.

"My good friends have come to see me!" he said. His voice was strong, and his eyes moved among the visitors from person to person as they all approached him.

"You had us worried for a little while, Mr. Rigsby," Frank began. "We've been praying for you, and we were really happy to hear that you might get to go home in a few days."

"Thank you, Frank, and I appreciate everyone's prayers. I have had excellent care here, but I am most *definitely* ready to return home. They tell me that it should happen at some point over the weekend."

Kate caught Frank's attention and nodded toward the books tucked under one arm. Frank held up the two books for him to see and then placed them on his bedside tray. "We brought these from your house for you."

"Oh, thank you so much. I hated to leave Mr. Churchill stranded in the War Cabinet room in the House of Commons." Leonard Rigsby winked at Kate.

The three boys looked at each other, unsure if their elderly friend was still dreaming. He tapped his slender finger on the cover of the thick biography. "But now I can help Winston get ready for the battles that are still to come," he said with a smile.

A nurse tapped on the door and entered the hospital room. "I need to interrupt and take this sweet gentleman's temperature and blood presure. Would you folks mind stepping aside for a few minutes?"

The group moved together away from the bed and waited until the nurse finished checking Mr. Rigsby's vital signs. As she gathered her equipment and moved toward the door, she thanked the boys and Kate for their patience, left the room, and the four friends approached the bed once again.

"Well, we don't want to stay long, Mr. Rigsby," Kate began. "Mostly, we just needed to see for ourselves that you are making progress here. The boys especially wanted to come with me."

"Don't feel like you need to hurry off. I don't have anything else on my agenda for today," he chuckled to himself as he raised his arms and gestured toward the door. "There isn't a line of people waiting in the hall to see me, I don't believe."

Griff took a step closer to the bed. "Mr. Rigsby, Chase and I went with Frank to your house last night to pick up those books. When we were about to go inside, we saw a light coming from your attic window, and then someone came down the steps and ran out the front door."

Kate's eyes widened as Griff spoke, and she turned her head toward Frank, lifting her shoulders and squinting her eyes as if to say, *"This is news to me!"*

Mr. Rigsby's smile faded, and a troubled expression filled his face. "Oh my goodness. Did you see who it was? Can you describe that man to me?"

"I'm afraid that it was dark, and all we could see was that he was big, and he might have been mostly bald. Then when he was running down the steps, he tripped and hurt his leg," Chase explained.

"We looked around the downstairs, and it didn't seem like he'd been anyplace but on the third floor," Frank explained. "We locked both doors when we left, but it looked to us like the man got inside by climbing the trellis and breaking a window into the attic along the back of the house."

Griff spoke next. "I don't believe he had been inside very long when we arrived."

"I'm sure that my dad can fix that window," Chase said.

"Is there anything really valuable up there—in your attic?" Frank asked.

Mr. Rigsby paused thoughtfully and looked past his guests into his hospital room before saying more. "It's mostly just dusty old things." He hesitated another few seconds before he spoke again. "Was Boyd... I mean, was the man carrying anything— when he left?"

Griff was first to reply. "Nothing that we could see, and his hands were probably empty because he shoved

Frank when he came through the attic door. To answer your question, I'd say 'no,' Mr. Rigsby."

"My, my, boys. Being there when you were, you probably prevented something much worse from happening. I'm sorry for the fright he gave you, but thank you for always being around to help me. I haven't gone into my attic since a few weeks after my wife passed away, and that was over eight years ago. I can barely even remember just what is stored up there."

•••••••

Kate drove the car out of the parking lot onto the highway, and then she turned to Frank. "I was a *little bit* surprised to hear just now about what happened with you three when you went to his house last night."

Griff quickly spoke from the back seat before Frank could respond to her. "I *tried* to tell my dad about it last night and again this morning. He was already asleep when I got home, and he had to be at City Hall before I went downstairs for breakfast."

"Yeah, and I'd planned to tell *my* dad as soon as Griff told *his* dad," Chase added.

"All right, then," Kate began, "I'm just thankful that none of you were hurt."

"Chase, I can unlock Mr. Rigsby's house for your dad with our spare key, but give me a heads up before that happens because I want to be there when he goes into the attic," Frank insisted.

"I'll check with him and see if he has time tonight after he closes the store," Chase said. "It won't take long for him to cut and install the new glass for the window."

They drove for another minute in silence, and then Frank said, "I believe that Mr. Rigsby was holding back on saying something just now. I can't imagine why, but he started to say someone's name and then stopped himself."

"Let's just add that to our list of the things we still don't know. Maybe we can figure it out soon," Griff said with a hopeful smile.

During the return to Lewisville, a mile outside of town, their car had just passed a sign that read *"Caution! Dangerous Curve Ahead!"* when Kate looked nervously into the rearview mirror.

"There's a truck coming up behind us, guys, and the driver keeps swerving across the center line!" Kate announced.

Everyone turned to see for themselves what Kate had noticed. A pickup truck behind them was rapidly closing the distance to their sedan. The person driving seemed to be having trouble controlling his vehicle. He veered left and right and, at times, crossed into the oncoming traffic lane. The trailer that the truck was towing teetered and leaned dangerously whenever the driver tried to return to his lane. Kate immediately realized that the driver had two choices—and both had bad outcomes.

"Brace yourselves because he's not stopping!" Kate yelled to the boys. *"He's either going to pass us or hit us!"*

Chapter 6

Chase was seated directly behind Frank, and when Kate yelled her warning, he instantly grabbed his seatbelt strap and pulled it tighter. He then turned around to see the speeding truck through the back window. *It was barely fifty feet away!* The expression on the driver's face seemed to be one of anger more than of fear. With a blind curve dead ahead, the truck driver yanked the steering wheel into the opposite lane to pass the boys and Kate. When the truck was alongside their car, Kate took her foot off the gas pedal and lightly pressed the brake. As their car slowed and the truck with its trailer raced ahead, Kate safely steered off the highway onto the gravel shoulder. She then brought the car to a complete stop, moved the gear selector into *Park* and loudly exhaled the breath she'd been holding.

The ordeal had lasted less than a half-minute, but time seemed to stand still for the passengers and Kate while it was underway. The tension in the car was high enough that no one spoke for another half-minute. Finally, Frank did what was on everyone's mind—he turned to face his sister and began to applaud. Chase and Griff joined him from the rear seats. Kate's face, which had been pale seconds earlier, began to brighten as the boys expressed their gratitude to her.

"Thank you, guys, but it wasn't me. God must've been protecting us because I was just trying hard to keep the steering wheel aimed ahead."

When they were back inside the town limits and the mood of those in the car had relaxed once again, Chase asked Kate, "Instead of taking us home, could you drop all of us off at my dad's store? I'll check and see if he can fix Mr. Rigsby's window *before* we eat supper. I've been noticing the clouds moving in, and rain would for sure get into the attic and ruin whatever is up there."

·······

Spencer's Hardware faced the two-blocks by one-block area of trees, park benches, sidewalks, and the bandstand that made up the town square. Chase's grandfather had initially opened the hardware store more than forty years earlier. When his grandfather's health worsened, Chase's dad took over its operation. The business was pleasant and well-stocked—a place that fascinated most children. It was also a favorite Saturday destination, especially for dads and their sons.

Kate slowed and then stopped along the curb in front of the store. Griff and Chase opened the back doors and got out first. Frank turned to Kate and said, "I have Mr. Rigsby's spare house key with me, and I've already clued mom in that I might not be home when you all start to eat supper. She said that would be fine. Thank you for being such a good driver, Sis." He leaned toward Kate and hugged her.

The boys pushed on the store's door, and the announcing bell attached to its top jingled on the metal spring. Charles Spencer was standing behind the counter with his back to them, mixing a can of paint for a customer.

"I'll be right with you," he said, unaware of who had entered.

"Take your time, Dad," Chase said. "We're just here to hang out until you close the store."

Mr. Spencer turned around and smiled at his oldest son. "Well, if that's the case, how about you grab a push broom in the back and sweep the aisles for me? And there's a trash can under the counter that could stand to be emptied. You'll find a second broom in the back room if Frank or Griff are interested."

"We'll be glad to help," Griff responded.

"As a thank you when you finish, there are some bottles of soda back there in the fridge," Chase's dad added, tipping his head in the direction of the storage room door.

The customer happened to be the final one of the day, and she paid for her paint and left while the three Bon Air boys cleaned the store. When they finished their work, Mr. Spencer invited them to enjoy their bottles of root beer while he locked the front door and counted the money in the cash register.

"So, to what do I owe the pleasure of you three young men gracing this humble store?" Mr. Spencer asked as he joined the boys in the storage room.

"Mr. Rigsby needs a windowpane replaced in his attic, and I thought that you wouldn't mind helping him," Chase said.

"It's supposed to rain later this evening, Mr. Spencer. Otherwise, it could probably wait until Saturday," Griff added.

"I'll be happy to do that. And do I understand correctly that Mr. Rigsby is still in the hospital?"

"He is, Dad. We just got back from visiting him. Kate took us there. He should be home in a few days," Chase replied.

"All of us would like to ride along with you when you go there to install the new glass—*if* you don't mind," Griff said.

"Of course. That's fine. Let me get some supplies together, and I'll drive us there in my truck."

"I have a key to open everything, Mr. Spencer," Frank remarked.

· · · · ·

Charles Spencer parked his pickup truck between the carriage house and the back porch. High over their heads, the tops of the maple, pine, and oak trees around the house and across the yard were beginning to sway ahead of the storm that was rapidly moving toward Lewisville.

"Let's go upstairs first so I can measure the opening of the broken window. I'll come back here and cut the correct piece of glass for it on my tailgate," Mr. Spencer suggested as they exited the vehicle.

Frank went into the house ahead of the others, and they quickly reached the attic stairway door. Mr. Spencer stepped ahead and was the first to climb the fourteen stairs, followed by Griff, Frank, and Chase.

The attic smelled like cedar shavings, old leather, and mothballs. A layer of dust coated everything in sight. Mr. Spencer crossed the room, unclipped the tape measure from his belt, and went to work at the broken window.

"Look at all of the footprints in the dust," Griff remarked to the other boys at a volume only they could hear. "You can see where that man went, and he went pretty much everywhere up here!"

"Yeah," Frank agreed, "and it looks like he especially spent time around this steamer trunk. Frank pointed to a large, old container made from wood and covered with thick black fabric. The trunk had two wide and cracked leather straps with buckles that held the trunk closed when it was transported by train or ship. The lid stood open, and many of its contents were spread on the attic floor. "Judging by the footprints in the dust, he was in this spot for a while," Frank guessed.

"Something up here must be *very* important to someone for them to risk climbing up that skinny trellis and then breaking a window to get in," Griff commented.

When he finished measuring the opening for the new pane of glass, Mr. Spencer pulled a small, spiral notebook and pen from his shirt pocket and jotted down the window dimensions. "I'll be right back, fellows. This won't take long."

Frank, Griff, and Chase slowly walked the length of the attic, examining the many items stored there. The wind by this time was whistling outdoors beyond the open window, and suddenly a cool gust of air rushed into the third floor. It toppled a dressmaker's dummy and pushed an antique hatbox onto the floor. Halfway across the room near the steamer trunk, a folded, light blue sheet of paper blew against Chase's shoe. He stooped to pick it up and then opened it. Chase studied the page, the only piece of paper scattered around the trunk that wasn't yellowed or brittle.

"Guys, come here! Look at this!" Chase moved a few feet so he could stand under a lightbulb with the paper. Frank and Griff came alongside him, and they each looked over a shoulder.

Chase described aloud what he'd found. "This is a rental agreement dated two days ago from a place over in Shelbyville! Whatever was rented only has item numbers on the page—there's no name or description of it. I can't make out the person's signature, but I recognize the name of the road in the address written down by whoever signed the receipt. It's a farm road northeast of town—one that intersects with the River Road!"

Frank could hardly contain his excitement. "We *have to* go there and check it out! This paper must have been dropped by that man when he was up here, and maybe..."

"*Shhh,* Frank! Chase, your dad's coming back. Put that paper in your pocket!" Griff said quietly. "We can talk about this later."

Charles Spencer finished replacing the broken pane of glass and then closed and locked the attic window, followed by the back door. The entire project had taken a half-hour. He dropped off Griff and Frank at their houses. At Frank's house, he put Chase's bicycle into the back of his pickup and then drove home with his son.

·······

"Breaker, breaker!" Griff was the first of the boys to call for the others on their walkie-talkies at 8:00. "Is anyone on?"

"I'm here!" Frank replied.

"Me, too!" Chase answered and continued. "Griff, have you told your dad the things we've learned?"

"Well, no—not yet, anyway. Before your dad drove us back from Mr. Rigsby's, my dad came home and ate an early supper because he had to go back out for a county commission meeting. I'll try to tell him tonight if I'm still awake when he gets home."

"I did a little bit of research using our telephone directory," Frank began, "and it looks like that place in Shelbyville mainly rents tractors, backhoes, and heavy equipment—the things you'd use on a farm or if you're in the construction business. It makes sense to me now that the address on that blue receipt is on a rural road out in the county."

"Why don't we go out there after lunch on Sunday and try to see if there is anything we can figure out before we tell my dad?" Griff suggested. "Waiting a few more days to mention all of this won't hurt.

Whether we *do* or *don't* learn anything new when we're there, at least after we go, we can give him a better picture of what we know for certain. Agreed?"

"I agree with you, Griff," Chase said.

"Okay, that's the plan for the weekend," Frank confirmed. "I'll see you guys Friday in homeroom."

· · · · · · ·

Griff was still awake when his dad returned from the county meeting. Lee Jenkins noticed his son's bedroom door was ajar and his bedside reading lamp was still on.

"Knock, knock," he said quietly as the Sheriff gently pushed the door open a few more inches. "Can I come in for a minute?" he asked Griff.

"Sure, Dad. I was just finishing up reviewing my Algebra for a quiz tomorrow, and I was about to turn off my light. How was your meeting?"

"Oh, it was okay. They mostly talked about things that don't concern my department or me, but I need to make an appearance whenever they schedule these things. The *biggest* fireworks of the night happened when the county supervisor fired one of the maintenance employees. I don't know the man, but apparently he has been in charge of the upkeep along the county roads. That means he's supposed to oversee picking up trash and mowing the grass between the roads and the private properties next to it—the right-of-way."

Griff had been reclining on his bed, propped up on two pillows holding his Algebra book on his chest. Upon hearing this, he put the book aside, raised on his elbows, and gave his dad his full attention.

"His supervisor said tonight that he regularly asked the man to mow all of the grass along the roads in the county, but he either forgets, or he doesn't get around to mowing some stretches of the right-of-way here and there. The folks who live on those roads have been complaining because they've been seeing rats and varmints coming out of the woods nearby. This has gone on for at least six months, so he lost his job tonight because his bosses said he was being insubordinate."

"What does that word 'insubordinate' mean, Dad?"

His father replied, "It means that the man won't obey his orders."

The more Lee Jenkins spoke, the faster Griff's heart beat.

"Do you remember his name—the man that was fired?"

"It was a Mr. Mueller. His first name, I believe, was Arnold—Arnold Mueller. He didn't handle the firing very well at all. He said some angry things and then kicked the door open when he left the room. But, that's enough about my evening. I won't keep you up any longer, son. You look very tired, and I just wanted to say goodnight, Griff. Sleep well, son."

As quickly as he'd arrived, his dad took a step back into the upstairs hallway and closed the bedroom door.

Only a moment earlier, Griff had struggled to keep his eyes open, trying to focus on his school book. Now, this news from his father immediately put his mind into fast motion!

The only section of right-of-way along the perimeter fence around the preserve that *hadn't* been mowed was where they had found the hidden entrance. Their spy camera's photograph showed a workman's truck with toolboxes. *Could it be that the person in boots and jeans standing by that truck was the man who was fired?* And if the three of them rode their bicycles to the address on the rental receipt, would they find that Arnold Mueller lived there? These questions and their possible answers kept Griff's mind racing until he finally drifted off to sleep shortly after eleven o'clock.

• • • • • • •

• *Friday* •

Griff arrived at school earlier than usual because he woke up long before his alarm clock had the chance to ring. He could hardly wait to tell Chase and Frank what he had learned from his dad the previous night—about Arnold Mueller and the county commission meeting.

When Chase walked into their homeroom, Griff motioned for him to hurry to Griff's desk.

"What do you think is the chance that your cousin Donnie would drive us out on River Road after school today?"

Chase lowered his backpack full of books onto his seat. "Donnie delivers newspapers starting around four o'clock. I don't know if he'd have time, but I can ask him, *if* I can get permission to use the telephone in the school office during our lunch break. But I thought we were going there on Sunday afternoon. Why do we suddenly need to go today?"

Frank arrived at that moment, dropped into his seat, and leaned toward his two friends. "Go where today?"

89

he asked Griff.

"I asked Chase if he thought Donnie could drive us after school today to the address on that rental receipt. I think we ought to go ahead and check out that house as soon as we can and maybe get a look at whoever lives there," Griff replied.

"Well, I'm available today even if Donnie isn't," Frank said and then smiled mischievously, "because you know how I *love* a good mystery!"

Griff spent the next few minutes telling his friends what his dad had mentioned from the county commissioner's meeting.

"So, what's your theory about all of this?" Frank asked when Griff finished speaking.

"I don't have a theory—not yet, anyway. And I also don't feel that we need to bother my dad with the things we've learned so far *unless* we can link someone in particular to the break-in at Mr. Rigsby's house."

"Yeah, let's try to hold off accusing anyone of anything until we've positively figured that the county guy was the one who broke into the attic," Chase agreed. "I'll try to call Donnie's house or at least leave a message with my aunt during our lunchtime."

· · · · · · ·

When the final school bell sounded, the Bon Air boys met at the bicycle rack in the rear parking lot.

"Donnie wasn't home when I made that phone call to him," Chase said. "Nobody answered at his house, so if we want to check out that address today, we'll have to get there on our own."

"It's not that far outside of town, anyway," Frank added. "We can do it."

Once the boys had coasted through the town square, they rode their bikes for ten minutes in single file farther out County Road 31. The route took them past the Lewisville Marina located off River Road. That road was also the county highway that ran alongside the New Haven River. The water of the New Haven on their left shimmered in the afternoon sunlight as it became visible in the distance from time to time between the trees. On their right were miles of telephone poles and train tracks. Before long, the three lanes of asphalt became two, and the road rose noticeably to a higher elevation. Fields and pastures filled the landscape beyond the railroad tracks.

Griff was in front of the others, and he looked over his should toward his friends. "We're coming up to the intersection with Thurman Road. We'll turn there."

Once they completed that turn, the boys passed a few homes here and there spaced far apart. "The address we're looking for is number 11375," Chase reminded his friends from the middle of the three bicycles.

In another half-mile, Griff slowed and said with a hushed voice over his shoulder, *"It's that gray house at the next driveway—the one with the big doghouse in the backyard."*

"And from here, I can see the name *Mueller* painted on the mailbox!" Chase added excitedly.

"Let's get away from the road, guys," Frank suggested. "We can move in closer and keep anyone from seeing us if we'll go on foot from here."

The house where they stopped had a *For Rent* sign

visible in a front window. The three of them walked their bicycles up its driveway and leaned them against the empty house. It was two hundred feet farther through unmowed grass and weeds to the gray house belonging to Arnold Mueller. A tan pickup truck was parked behind the gray house close to the back porch. An oversized and detached garage that was big enough to be a small barn was thirty yards behind the house, positioned near a line of trees.

"I can't tell from this angle if there are any toolboxes on that truck or not," Griff whispered as he crouched low to the ground in the shadow of the empty house.

"Let's just stay here for a few minutes and watch to see if anyone comes or goes," Chase suggested. As they waited, they squatted low and then duck-walked to an area in the tall grass halfway between the two houses.

Not long after getting into that position, the rear screen door of the gray house swung open, and a man appeared on the porch. Following the sound the door made when it slammed behind him, a pit bull bolted out of the doghouse toward the man. A heavy chain attached to the dog's collar stretched tightly. That chain stopped the brown and white dog, and it began to bark wildly. The man on the porch held up a large soup bone and tossed it underhanded to the barking dog. The homeowner, unlike the man who ran out of Mr. Rigsby's house, was short, broad-chested, and had a full head of gray hair.

A gust of wind blew from behind the boys and toward the Mueller house. Suddenly the pit bull seemed to lose interest in the bone. He lifted his head and sniffed the scent of unfamiliar humans carried on the breeze from the boys' hiding place. The large dog then began to walk toward them, dragging his chain and holding his nose high. The stocky animal began to whine and whimper as it stretched out the entire length of the chain so much that the pit bull eventually stood on its hind legs with its muzzle pointing directly toward the boys. The man on the porch walked down the steps and stood behind the dog, which by this time was pulling fiercely on his leash, barking non-stop, and lunging toward the boys' hiding place!

Chapter 7

Fear of being discovered gripped Chase, Frank, and Griff, and they dropped flat to the ground. They hoped the gray-haired man hadn't seen them. At almost the same time, they realized that the breeze which took their scent to the dog would also carry their voices. So, to communicate, Griff made hand signals to the others, and the three of them began to army crawl back to the vacant house.

In a moment, they heard the distant low hum of a gas-powered motor, and it grew louder with every second. The boys recognized it as an airplane engine, and in no time at all, its volume rose to a deafening level! They caught a glimpse of a crop duster less than a hundred feet away, flying slowly over the planted field next to them. It was so close to the ground they felt they could have reached up to touch it! The boys had not noticed until then the dozens of acres of corn planted beyond the border of trees. The corn's light green stalks stretched for hundreds of yards to the left and right behind the houses along Thurman Road.

"Let's hope that pilot stays close to here for a while," Griff said with his hands cupped to his mouth as he tried to speak over the drone of the engine. *"Whatever he is spraying on that field ought to cover our scent, and the noise the plane is making should help us get away from here."*

·······

On Saturday morning, when Wayne Whidden tapped on his son's bedroom door and spoke Frank's name, he heard no response. He turned the knob, slowly pushed the door open, and found Frank still sleeping soundly. His eyes were shut, but his mouth was open, and he was hugging his pillow. The bedspread had become flipped sideways across the young teenager, who was positioned with his left leg on the bed and his right foot dangling off the edge.

"Frank. *Frank!* It's time to wake up."

Frank groaned and then mumbled through his dry mouth, "'Okay. Mornin' Dad."

"Good morning, son. I came upstairs to tell you that Patrick Wilson just called from a payphone outside Fort Everett."

Frank raised his head and shoulders and looked toward the open door as he tried to focus his sleepy eyes on the familiar figure standing there.

His father continued, "Kate said she told you that Patrick Wilson called me the other day to see if he could come visit us today instead of Sunday. He said just now that he was planning to stop for breakfast along the way, but we insisted that he come straight here and eat with us. So, he's on his way here and should be arriving in fifteen or twenty minutes. He wanted to know if you would like to go hiking with him in the preserve, and I told him I thought you probably would."

Frank stretched his arms, yawned, kicked off his bedspread, swung his legs off the bed as he sat up, and placed both feet on the floor. He rubbed his eyes and blinked them mostly open.

"Gosh, Dad, I'd love that!"

"I mentioned to him about your friends Chase and Griff, and he said you could feel free to invite them to join the two of you."

"All right, then. I'll throw on some clothes, head downstairs, and give them a call," Frank said, *this* time becoming more clear-minded and sounding like himself.

"Mom will have breakfast ready to go on the table fairly soon, so please hurry," Mr. Whidden requested as he closed his son's bedroom door. Seconds later, he opened it again. "Oh, and I thought you'd be glad to know that Mr. Rigsby is being discharged from the hospital later this morning. Your mother, Kate, and I are driving over to get him after we all have breakfast."

"That's great, Dad! Tell him that I'll be glad to help him around his house anywhere he needs me."

Mr. Whidden closed the bedroom door a second time. Frank stood and dressed in the jeans he had draped over his desk chair on Friday night. He pulled a light blue t-shirt over his head, dragged three fingers through his hair, and planted a Lewisville Lions baseball cap on his head. Frank then slipped into a pair of low-quarter sneakers from his closet, tied their laces, and headed for the kitchen.

"Morning, Mom. Everything smells incredible!" Frank said as he eyed the bowl of cut-up cantaloupe pieces, the stack of crispy bacon slices, a basket of biscuits, and the steaming bowl of grits.

"Good morning, Frank." She turned as he came up behind his mom, and she placed a quick kiss on his cheek. "I hope you've come downstairs hungry because there will be plenty of food."

"Don't worry about me! Anything you fix is always the best!"

He picked up the receiver of the wall-mounted telephone and dialed Griff's number. While he waited for someone to answer, Mrs. Whidden whispered, *"Invite him to join us if he hasn't already eaten his breakfast."*

Frank nodded to his mother, and within a few moments, both Chase and Griff had accepted the breakfast invitations and the offers to join him and Patrick for some hiking inside the preserve.

Frank put plates, forks and knives, juice glasses, and paper napkins at the seats around the dining room table. He removed a pitcher of chilled orange juice and a butter dish from the refrigerator, and he set them in the center of the table. Finally, he placed a jar of strawberry preserves and a jar of apple butter next to the juice pitcher.

Chase and Griff entered the house together and stood around in the kitchen visiting with Mr. Whidden while everyone waited for the young Army corporal to arrive. In a few minutes, the morning sun's light glinted off a red car's windshield, flashing a quick beam across the living room wall. Frank saw it and realized that the soldier had just arrived. He left the conversation with his friends to open the front door and greet Patrick Wilson.

"It's great to see you again!" Frank said as he opened his arms to wrap a bear hug around Patrick.

"I've been counting the days this week until I could come back here and be with your family," Patrick said.

When their guest had barely come through the door, Frank's collie happily ran to their visitor. Then he and his collie friend enjoyed a moment of reunion that included a half-minute of belly rubs for Duke.

Once everybody came together in the dining room, Wayne Whidden introduced Chase and Griff to Patrick. Then he offered a prayer of thanks for the meal, as well as for the friends standing around the table.

Thirty minutes after breakfast began, the plates and platters were emptied of food. The Bon Air boys quickly cleared the table so their outing with Patrick could get underway.

"If there is room in the back of the car, could you take your microphone and tape recorder with you today?" Kate asked her brother and Patrick. "Since we had to cut our Sunday afternoon trip short, there are still a few bird types that I'd like to try to get recorded onto your equipment."

Frank turned to Patrick and gave him a look that asked for his permission. "Sure! That's no problem," Patrick said. "The only things in my trunk are a spare tire and a toolbox, so I have plenty of room for it."

"Thanks! Mom and Dad asked me to go with them for the next hour or two," Kate explained. "After we get Mr. Rigsby settled again at his house, I'll drive down to the preserve and meet you four. Frank, if you'll take your walkie-talkie with you, I'll bring the extra one with me and call you on it when I arrive there."

•••••••

As they drove to the south side of Lewisville, Patrick told his three passengers about his growing-up years in Wyoming before he joined the Army. He lived on a small ranch, which backed up to the Teton Mountain range. As a teenager, Patrick spent as much time as possible in the forests and the foothills near his home. He said that he was just as comfortable riding a horse as most people are riding a bicycle. Patrick was telling about a wintertime cross-country skiing trip he had made with his father when they arrived at the preserve gate and the caretaker's house.

"All of this property belongs to a family friend," Frank explained. "I've been wondering how you first heard about the preserve. I don't think they advertise this place, do they?"

"A guy in my barracks at Fort Everett was an avid hunter growing up, and one day he told me about the huge bucks that are all over a place he called 'the preserve.' He explained that no hunting of any kind is allowed there, but he said if you ever tracked down a deer with 16-point or even 12-point antlers at a regular hunting camp, you might pay as much as $5,000 for the privilege of shooting one of those. And he said there are *many* deer that large in the preserve. I've seen several of them here, myself."

Patrick parked in front of the padlocked gate and turned off the car's motor. As he opened his door, he said, "You guys can wait here while I ask Mr. Denton to let us go in."

The boys watched Patrick walk to the small house. After ringing the doorbell, he took a step back and waited for the caretaker. In a half-minute, they saw the door open. The large man appeared in the doorway wearing faded blue jeans and a sleeveless t-shirt. There was a vertical split going halfway up one of his pants legs. They couldn't hear the conversation, but Patrick's expression and posture changed after several seconds, telling the boys that something was wrong. Mr. Denton pushed the screen door open even more and stepped toward Patrick. Patrick stood nearly six feet in height, but the caretaker was several inches taller. Six days earlier, Mr. Denton had been able to walk between the house and cars with no problems. Today, however, the big man moved slowly, supporting himself with one crutch, and he had a white plaster cast that began at his right knee and went down to his toes!

After several seconds of conversation, Patrick returned to his car. Mr. Denton turned around and disappeared into his house.

"He told me he can't let us go in today," the young soldier said as he inserted his key into the car's ignition switch and started the engine.

"*Can't* or *won't*?" Chase asked from the rear seat.

Patrick placed the car into reverse and turned partway around in his seat.

"It sounded like some of both. Mr. Denton said that he'd heard from 'a Mr. Miller' who told him to keep the preserve closed through the end of the day."

"Was it Mr. *Miller* or *Mueller*?" Griff questioned.

"Yeah, Mueller was the name. That was it! He told me that Mr. Mueller phoned him last night with those instructions. That's all he would say about him."

Frank turned around in his seat and faced toward Griff and Chase. "Did that fellow—Mr. Denton—look familiar in a different sort of way to either of you? Because, to me, something—actually *several* things— aren't adding up."

"Yeah, especially that cast on his leg," Griff said confidently. "It looked like it was a new one. He didn't have that on his leg when we came on Sunday. I would have noticed it."

"And that Mueller person must be the same one your dad told you about—the man that was fired by the county," Frank said to Griff. "How can he shut down someone else's property, anyway?"

"I'm just really sorry that you guys got up early to come here with me, and then we got turned away," Patrick said as he backed his car into position to leave. "If you want to, we can drive over to Perry State Park, but the trails there aren't in good shape. It's not being maintained very well these days."

"No, Patrick, let's not do that," Griff suggested. He paused and looked at Chase and Frank before he said more. "We haven't told anyone else about this, but there's another way to get into the preserve." He paused and then Griff pointed forward to the driveway. "When you get back out to the highway, turn right. We'll show you something that the three of us discovered."

"Yeah," Frank added. "We think there's more going on here than certain people would probably like *other* people to know about."

When their car reached the intersection with the county road, Patrick followed Griff's instructions and turned right. A half-mile ahead, Patrick turned right again and drove another mile to the rear corner of the preserve. The hidden gate was about one hundred yards away off to their right.

Before Patrick began to turn the corner and drive ahead, Frank glanced out his side passenger window and saw the rear end of a vehicle passing through the hidden gate. The red taillights glowed for a brief second when the driver pressed his brake pedal, and then the vehicle—a truck—disappeared from view.

Patrick saw the same thing as Frank, but didn't understand the importance of what had just happened.

"Wait!" Frank quickly held up his left hand and reached for the steering wheel, signaling Patrick not to proceed. Chase and Griff watched Frank's concern from the back seat as he stared intently along the fence line. "A pickup truck just went through the gate," Frank said. "Now I see somebody's arms and hands. He's lowering the rolled-up fence." Another thirty seconds passed, then Frank said, "I guess whoever that person is, he's staying inside the property for now."

Frank turned to Patrick and the two buddies behind him. "Let's look for a place to park where we won't be seen—a place like..."

They all scanned the few houses that were spread out widely around their location. The one nearest to them was the gutted one that had damage to the roof from a fallen tree limb. It was a few hundred feet from the others.

"Let's go there and park behind that house," Frank suggested as he pointed. "Whoever went into the preserve just now wouldn't be able to see us from that spot, and we can lay low and watch to see if anybody comes or goes."

"All right, but you guys will *have to* explain to me whatever it is *you* know that *I* don't," Patrick urged.

"It's kind of a long story, but we think something illegal is going on inside the preserve," Chase began.

"And if it isn't illegal, it sure seems sneaky!"

Patrick slowly drove the length of the weed-filled and bumpy gravel driveway until they were behind the abandoned house. "Frank told me about the men he heard making a plan or sounding suspicious back behind the trees. He showed me his invention when I went to his house with Duke on Sunday night."

Chase continued, "Well, there are a couple of separate coincidences, and we can't say for sure how they might connect. First, Mr. Rigsby, the person who owns all of the preserve property, has had his house broken into. We don't know if that break-in is what they were planning on the recording Frank made or if there's still something else coming."

"Yeah," Griff said, "the next thing is that in the attic where the man broke a window to get inside, we found a receipt for something that was rented—some kind of big piece of equipment."

Chase spoke again. "Then back on Monday, we put a little camera by that gate over there, and Griff developed and printed the film from it. The camera snapped a photo of a truck with toolboxes mounted along the back, and it showed the bottom half of a man wearing work boots."

Patrick Wilson began to laugh. "You three guys sound like Perry Mason, Sherlock Holmes, and Joe Friday from *Dragnet*! I am amazed at what you've figured out in just the last few days! So, what'll we do now—just park here and wait?"

"I think so—at least for the moment." Frank put his hand on the door handle. "Can you unlock your trunk? I want to try to use my microphone and listen for anything that might be going on inside the preserve with whoever went just went through the gate."

All of them got out of the car and gathered around the trunk. Frank removed his portable tape recorder and put its strap across one shoulder. He rested the headphones around his neck and then plugged the microphone cable into the recorder. Frank smiled at the others and patted the lid of the device. "Fresh batteries and a new reel of tape!"

They moved cautiously to a rear corner of the abandoned house and peered around the edge. "I'll go ahead of you, Frank, and make sure it's clear—that nobody is in sight," Griff suggested.

Griff walked along the side of the house behind overgrown bushes until he reached the front corner. From there, he scanned across the area where the vehicle had entered. When he saw and heard no one in either direction on the road, he turned around and motioned for Frank to come ahead.

Frank placed the headphones over his ears, switched on his tape recorder, and walked forward in the tall weeds and grass until he was next to Griff. Supporting his device with both hands, Frank pointed the dish toward the trees that lined the property inside the chain-link fence. He slowly swept the microphone back and forth while listening for any human sound. Almost immediately, he said, "There's some sort of metal-against-metal scraping noise... and now a car door has closed." Frank stared ahead in silence. "Another car door just closed. They've started the engine." Frank paused longer this time. "It's getting closer and louder now. *I think they're coming toward us!*"

Both Frank and Griff turned around and nearly sprinted back to the rear of the abandoned house. As they ran, their eyes locked on to Chase and Patrick, who had been watching the two and waiting for details. *"They're on the move back in the preserve!"* Frank said as he and Griff reached the others.

"What's going on?" Chase asked. "What did you hear?"

"Some noises like metal clanking, car doors being shut, and an engine starting up."

"Let's move to where we can watch them if they come back through the gate," Griff said.

"Be careful, guys," Patrick said. "I feel responsible that we're here, and I sure don't want anyone getting hurt."

From behind bushes on both corners at the front of the house, they saw a tan truck drive directly toward them, coming from the trees and shadows into the sunlight. It stopped at the closed gate. The mirrors on either side of the truck cleared two pine trees by less than a foot as the vehicle eased between them and into view. It was the tan truck they had seen at the gas station while waiting to put air in Chase's bicycle tire. And it was the same one that appeared in the photo from Chase's camera!

The passenger, someone none of them recognized, opened his door, got out, and pulled on a rope that ran to the top of the fence and over two pulleys. The chainlink gate rolled up, and the vehicle passed by under it. The driver continued inching forward when, into the full sunlight, there appeared a covered horse trailer hitched to the truck!

"Wow!" was all Griff could say as he looked at Patrick. Frank and Chase stared at the sight from behind the bushes with new questions and few answers. They had the same thought: What is all of this about?

After the passenger lowered the chain-link gate to the ground and returned to his seat, the truck and trailer bounced and rocked through the tall grass until the vehicles reached the road. The driver eased carefully onto the asphalt and, once there, he pushed the gas pedal to the floor. Mud spun off the rear tires, and a trail of gray exhaust spiraled out of the pickup's tailpipes. The men were obviously in a hurry; however, they had no idea that four pairs of watchful eyes had just seen them drive away from the preserve.

Chapter 8

When the truck and trailer were almost out of sight, the Bon Air boys and Patrick left the front of the abandoned house and walked back to the car.

"What do we do now?" Chase asked the group, supposing that one of them had a plan in mind.

Patrick raised the trunk lid so Frank could put his microphone device back into it, and while the trunk was open, Frank removed his walkie-talkie.

"We could try to follow the truck, but in the direction it was headed, there are three or four different turnoffs they could take. We'd never find them," Griff said confidently.

"What *I* want to do is see whatever is back in there where they just came from," Chase said.

"I'm going to leave you guys for a minute to call Kate on the walkie-talkie and tell her not to come," Frank said as he pulled the radio's antenna to its full length. "Since the preserve is shut down today, it would be a waste of her time." He stepped away from the others while his friends continued their discussion.

"Since we're already here, let's go into the property through their gate and look around," Chase said. "If the truck comes back while we're behind the fence, there will be lots of places where we can get out of sight."

•••••••

Frank finished his radio conversation with Kate and walked across the road to join the others.

"Kate just told me some bad news. A few minutes ago, my sister and my parents got to Mr. Rigsby's house after picking him up from the hospital. They discovered that someone had broken the glass in his back door and had gone into his house. They're now trying to figure out if anything is missing. She asked if we could leave here soon and help them check everything out."

"We can always come back to the preserve later. There's plenty of time left in the day," Griff said to Frank, and then he turned to Patrick. "Do you mind? Can you drive us back to town now?"

"That's fine. Yeah, we can go," Patrick said.

The four of them took their seats in the car, Patrick proceeded carefully down the gravel driveway to the road, and before long, they turned onto Goldstone Lane, where Leonard Rigsby lived.

When they reached the house, they noticed a truck and two cars parked near the rear porch.

"Pull in here, Patrick, and then stop next to the carriage house," Frank directed. "Those must be the people delivering the hospital bed. Yeah, I recognize the men from church."

Patrick brought his car to a stop and the four of them got out. "It is nice to be in a place where folks help each other like this," Patrick commented. "Where I come from, people stay to themselves, and you don't see this sort of kindness between neighbors."

Frank smiled. "That's Lewisville for you! Some amazing people live here, and they love to serve and help each other."

As they climbed the steps and reached the back door, their shoes crunched the broken glass fragments scattered on the cement porch.

"I'll go find a broom and a dustpan and get this cleaned up," Chase offered as he hurried his pace and walked into the house ahead of the others.

Mrs. Whidden passed Chase in the doorway as she came onto the porch. "Deputy Martin just left here. He dusted the doorknob looking for fingerprints, but he didn't find anything usable. He guesses that it was probably the work of a random person passing through town."

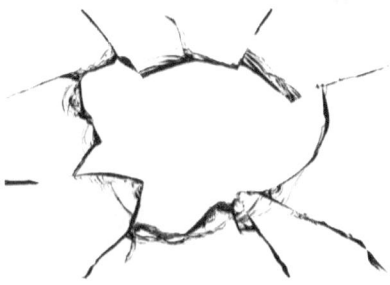

Frank shot a glance at Griff. Griff raised his eyebrows but didn't say anything as a response.

"Does Mr. Rigsby seem upset, Mom, because I want to talk with him about this," Frank said as his mother took a step back inside the house. The two Bon Air boys and Patrick followed her into the kitchen.

"He seems fine. He is in the parlor visiting with your father and Kate," she replied.

Chase came toward them carrying a broom and dustpan. "I'll sweep up this mess and then join you guys in a minute," he said.

In the parlor, Leonard Rigsby was seated in a

richly padded chair, the back of which rose a foot higher than the top of his head. The chair made him seem even smaller with his slight frame and narrow shoulders. When Griff, Frank, and Patrick entered the room, the elderly gentleman's eyes opened wide, and a smile spread across his face. Frank's dad stood and his mother stepped alongside him as the newcomers arrived. Wayne Whidden said, "We don't want to overwhelm you with so many people here, so Mrs. Whidden and I will be going now. It looks like the men from church are getting your bed ready. Kate will be with you for most of the afternoon and make sure that you get a good supper. Judging by the smells coming from the kitchen, I'd say that your lunch is about ready. The ladies from our church have lined everything up for your meals during the next two weeks. A volunteer will bring them to you each morning."

Frank's mother added, "And I can assure you that you *won't* starve." Everyone laughed.

Mr. Whidden continued, "Frank and his buddies can help with anything you need from them. And be sure to get to know *this* young man, our newest friend." He pointed to Patrick. "If he'd let us adopt him, we would. His name is Patrick Wilson, and he's from Fort Everett." After saying those things, Frank's parents and Kate left the room.

Patrick smiled and raised a hand as he gave a slight wave and said, "It's a pleasure to meet you, sir."

Leonard Rigsby lifted his right hand to his forehead and offered a salute. "It is *my* pleasure, son. Thank you for serving our country."

Chase joined them as Frank stepped forward to

speak. "Mr. Rigsby, this makes twice in less than a week that someone has broken into your house. Do you have any idea why they're doing this now or what they might be looking for?"

The gentleman motioned for them to take their seats near him in the parlor. "I don't like to talk about this," Leonard Rigsby began, "but I'm afraid that I *do* know why—at least I *think* I do. I believe all of this is because of property my wife inherited from her family more than forty years ago. Her parents died eleven months apart back then. It was their land at the time, and it had belonged to *her* father's family long before their deaths."

"The nature preserve?" Chase asked.

"Yes, that's right. While my wife was alive, there wasn't any problem for us concerning the ownership because it was clearly hers as the only living heir of her parents when they passed on. But when my wife died eight years ago, one of her nephews began to pester me, saying that the property should have been sold and the money divided between him and a second nephew. They were the sons of my wife's deceased sisters. The two of them said that it wasn't proper for me to keep the ownership of it."

"That doesn't seem right, Mr. Rigsby," Griff said. "If it was hers, it was hers to keep or do with whatever she wanted."

"I agree with you, Griff," Mr. Rigsby continued. "The problem with all of this concerns the deed for the land." He paused and looked at each boy and Patrick. "*I don't have it*—at least I don't know where it is. I accidentally let that information slip a few months ago when Boyd—that's one of the nephews—Boyd Abbott—when Boyd came here to see me. I said I couldn't help him because I couldn't put my hands on the deed."

"Do you mean that there's a chance he could find it and take the preserve away from you?" Frank asked.

"News travels fast in a small town, Frank, and when people learned that I went into the hospital on Sunday, well, you saw what happened with the attic window and now the back door. I believe that they thought I might not recover and they would have an opportunity to take control of the preserve property."

"Yes, sir," Frank said, "it didn't take long for the bad guys to show up!"

"The person we saw—the one who broke the attic window—spent his time upstairs, and it looked to us that nothing down here was bothered. Do you think the deed is somewhere up there?" Chase asked.

If I had to start looking for it, that's where I would begin, Chase," Leonard Rigsby replied. "I wish that I could be more helpful. There's a collection of so many old things in my attic that it won't be easy for anyone to find the deed, and I guess that's a *good* thing—at least, I hope so. As long as I'm alive, I don't believe the preserve land will be in jeopardy of falling into either nephew's hands. But if Boyd finds and holds the deed, he can try to make claims that might tie up the title for the land in court for months or years."

"We *can't* let that happen," Frank said. "If the deed is upstairs in the attic, we'll find it!"

"Right now, Mr. Rigsby, something is happening at the preserve, and I don't believe you would approve of it," Griff reported. "The caretaker closed the gate today and locked it." He nodded toward the young soldier. "Patrick normally comes into town on weekends, and he enjoys hiking the trails there..."

"That's precisely how I want the land to be kept available and used," Mr. Rigsby interrupted. "I want people to enjoy God's gift to us—the beauty of nature. Those are my instructions to Mr. Denton, and I pay him to keep the entrance and parking areas safe and secure so small groups of people can reserve days and times to go there to hike, picnic, and enjoy it."

"Well, this morning, when we went there hoping to go hiking, Mr. Denton said that a person named Mueller told him to keep the gate locked today," Griff said.

Mr. Rigsby stiffened and sat higher in his chair. He lowered his voice, and his eyes narrowed. "*Arnold Mueller*? That man is a *bad* influence around this town. He is *trouble* with a capital 'T,' and he has always been that way!"

"What we saw there this morning makes us think that a couple of men have something in mind that you wouldn't like—something to do with taking deer or some wildlife out of the property in a trailer. We would like to go back there and try to confirm these things so that we can report them to my dad," Griff said forcefully.

"Do we have your permission to speak for you, Mr. Rigsby?" Frank asked.

"*Yes*, son. Yes, you do. Just be careful. I don't know how far Boyd Abbott and any others might go to carry out their plans to take the preserve away from me."

·······

Patrick and the three boys planned to return to the secret gate and watch for anyone coming or going, but they stayed with Mr. Rigsby during the next forty-five minutes. He insisted that they share lunch from the generous tray of sandwiches, potato salad, a bowl of cut fruit, and homemade brownies the two church ladies had brought to him.

By 1:00, they returned to the property and reached the perimeter road along the back of the preserve. Once again, Patrick had parked his car out of sight behind the same abandoned house. The four of them walked through the front yard to the edge of the road and checked their surroundings. None of them saw or heard any evidence of traffic or people, so they dashed across the road, through the tall grass, and dropped to their knees in front of the chain-link gate. The uncut weeds along the right-of-way hid them from any passing cars while they considered their next move.

"I can lift the bottom of the gate and hold it up so you guys can go in first," Patrick said.

"Then I'll hold it up for you to come in," Griff offered.

Once inside, they walked quickly into the shade and shelter of the trees. The rain that had fallen overnight left the ground soft. The tire tracks that had been made earlier were easy to follow as they snaked their way into the distance through gaps between trees."

"Let's keep away from the ruts the truck and trailer made," Patrick suggested. "We don't need to put our footprints anywhere into the wet ground around those tire tracks. In my Army survival training, we learned things like that. There's no need to tell your enemies where we have been."

"How about if we split up into teams of two?" Frank suggested. Both can follow the truck path, but one team stays over on one side, the others go to the other side," Frank suggested. "We can cover more ground that way and be on the lookout for whatever seems out of the ordinary."

"That's a great idea, Frank," Patrick agreed. "None of us can be sure that there isn't another person or more people still hiding in the woods. We saw a truck leave, and it looked like two men were in it. That's all we know for sure."

"Chase and Griff," Frank began, "you two go to the left, and Patrick and I will stay to the right. Let's just keep walking until we get to where the tire ruts end."

"Try to keep the others in your view, and use bird calls instead of words if you need to get the attention of anyone," Patrick suggested. "That's also from my survival training," he said with a smile.

"Griff does an excellent imitation of a Grey-headed chickadee," Chase said with a wink.

"Fine! And you can do your famous crow call!" Griff teased as everyone chuckled. He wagged his head, smiled, and rolled his eyes.

"Onward, guys!" Frank insisted, hoping to unify his friends. "We have a mission we need to accomplish, so keep your eyes open!"

The Bon Air boys and Patrick spread out and slowly moved farther into the preserve. The canopy of trees grew thicker the farther into the preserve they went. Chase walked faster than the others and was twenty-five yards ahead of them when he suddenly signaled his friends with the sound of a crow! The other three froze and turned toward him. Chase motioned for them to come closer, and in a moment, the four of them stood looking at the contraption he had discovered.

The metal object was a cage made from heavy wire. It was about six feet tall, eight feet long, and four feet wide. Vines had grown up its sides, and on top of it were many small limbs covered with brown leaves—apparently placed there to camouflage it. The open end of the cage was tall enough and wide enough that the boys could walk into it by barely ducking. On the bottom of the cage were kernels of dried corn sprinkled from the opening to the closed end. Farthest from the entrance—about a foot above the ground was a tripwire stretched between the two sides. When an animal eating the corn bumped the tripwire, a rolled-up curtain of chain-link material was loaded and ready to drop behind the animal, instantly trapping it.

"There's no question about what *this* is," Patrick said. "Someone has put this cage here to capture whitetail deer or even the larger bucks."

"Do you all think this is supposed to be here—to control the deer herd on purpose?" Chase asked the group.

"I don't know," Frank replied. "We ought to ask Mr. Denton what it's here for and who checks it for deer?"

"The way this thing is covered in leaves and vines, I'm amazed that Chase noticed it!" Griff commented. "But let's keep going forward. It's only going to get darker in here the longer we stay."

They continued walking on either side of the path

made by truck tires on the scrub grass and pine needles. Wherever limbs had fallen onto the trail, someone had pulled them aside, clearing the way for the vehicle to go forward. Where a large tree stood in the way, the well-worn truck path simply detoured around it.

They soon reached a clearing wide enough for a skilled truck driver to use for a turnaround. It was there that they made their next discovery. It was a four-sided animal pen outlined by six-foot tall rough-cut wooden poles on the sides and the corners. Three lengths of barbed wire at different heights were strung around and nailed to the posts. A makeshift gate of wire was stretched across the opening. A metal box was located on the ground about twenty-five feet from one of the corner posts. A tan wire ran between the box and the barbed wire of the pen. Patrick lifted the lid of the box and announced, "Guys, there are a bunch of big truck batteries in here. And they're connected to the barbed wire. *Someone has put electricity for a fence charger here to keep animals inside the pen!*"

They all stood silently, looking at the crude corral. Frank finally spoke.

"There is no way that all of this is *supposed* to be here—I mean *officially* here. The preserve is where the animals are expected to run free. A pen like this to hold them—to keep them in such a little space—that's the opposite of what Mr. Rigsby would want, and it's just plain cruel!"

"I agree with you, Frank," Patrick said. "It looks like these guys must be tracking and capturing the prize bucks—those *expensive* ones—here inside the preserve. That's all I can figure with a setup like this."

"The poachers probably force the deer into this pen and hold them until they can tranquilize them and then deliver them to a buyer," Chase guessed. "That must be what the trailer is for."

"Fellows, I would like to stay here and get to the bottom of this mystery," Patrick stated, "but I think we should be heading back into town. We've made a big discovery, but your families are probably wondering if *I* kidnapped you or something." He laughed, and the others chuckled at that thought.

"All right, Patrick," Griff agreed. "But it's actually more like *we* kidnapped *you!*"

"That's true," Frank nodded. "We appreciate you bringing us here. Finding that cage and the pen explains a lot of what we've been wondering."

The four of them turned toward the road and began to walk in silence in the direction of the gate. Suddenly, in mid-step, Patrick stretched out both arms and signaled for the boys to stop. He put a single finger to his lips.

"Shhh! Listen!" he whispered. Everyone froze and strained to hear something other than the forest sounds. "It's an engine—straight ahead!" Patrick said.

In the distance toward the road, perhaps an eighth of a mile away, a windshield reflected the rays of sunlight with a flash into their eyes. A vehicle was approaching from directly in front of them, and unless the boys and Patrick found places to hide, they would undoubtedly be discovered!

"Get off the path!" Patrick whispered urgently. He pointed to their right, "Chase and Griff, you two head into those trees and get as close to the ground as you

can." He pointed in the other direction. "Frank, follow me this way!"

He and Frank dashed to the left, and they vaulted over fallen trees and trunks as they scanned the forest for anything big enough to hide them.

Chase and Griff separated, sprinting away from the tire ruts. The part of the forest where they found themselves was flatter, and it had even fewer fallen trees. When Griff saw a suitable place to take cover, he jumped and leaned to his side, threw his legs forward, and slid like a baseball player reaching home plate, stopping against a stack of tree limbs.

Chase was fifty feet away from the truck path and had just seen Griff slide when *he* hurdled over the trunk of a fallen tree. But instead of Chase's sneakers landing on the forest floor, the ground seemed to swallow him as he dropped into a hole, and everything around him suddenly went black!

Chapter 9

The truck pulling the trailer came very close to the boys' hiding places, passed between the two groups of them, and then continued ahead toward the barbed wire pen. When it was fully out of sight, Griff, Frank, and Patrick cautiously returned to the muddy truck path where they met.

"Where's Chase?" Frank asked Griff. "Didn't the two of you hide together?"

"No. Chase split away from me, and I figured he did the same thing I did—found some branches or a log and got behind them."

Patrick didn't wait for more discussion about the missing friend. *"Come on, guys!"* he said in an anxious whisper over his shoulder as he began to walk away. "We need to spread out and find him! Move out next to me in a straight line and stay about twenty feet apart. Then walk away from the truck path for fifty or sixty feet. I don't believe Chase would have gone farther into the woods than that. Just keep looking around and down into the leaves and branches in case he fell somewhere. He might have hit his head. Keep an eye out for his red shirt. Since we can't really call out for him, listen for any sounds he might be making. He could be really hurt."

They made their first sweep of the area walking away from the path. Then they turned around, shifted twenty-five or thirty feet to their right and began to walk again in the opposite direction. The three were careful to move silently, not wanting the sounds of small limbs and leaves under their feet to give away their presence. Halfway back to the truck path, Frank suddenly stopped. He noticed something red moving at ground level, and then he saw Chase's head and shoulders. He was struggling to pull himself out of a hole.

"How about a hand from somebody?" Chase said in a loud whisper. "There's not much down here to hold on to."

Griff and Frank hurried to the edge of a manmade rectangular hole, got on their knees, and extended their arms and hands to Chase.

"You fell into an old pit trap—the kind I've seen used to catch wolves or pigs," Patrick noted as he joined them. "You can tell that it hasn't caught anything for a while because the camouflage—the branches and leaves that covered over its top—those are still mostly in place except where you fell in."

Chase brushed muddy dirt from his jeans and stomped caked mud off his shoes. "All I did was jump over a big log, and I landed on that covering over the hole," he explained. "It looked like a bunch of leaves, but I went straight down through some sticks. When I hit the bottom, it knocked the wind out of me. It's gotta be at least six feet deep—maybe more."

"You're lucky that you didn't break anything," Frank commented. "It looks like it was pretty muddy down there, huh?"

Chase used both hands and continued to fling dirt clods from his jeans. "Yeah, it was *definitely* that!"

"We saw the truck and trailer go by, and it kept on heading toward that electric deer pen," Griff said. "I think we should try to sneak in closer and see what those guys are up to."

"I agree, Griff," Patrick said, "but we absolutely can't make a sound! They might have weapons with them."

"Be sure to step toe first, then heel, just like the Native Americans did," Frank said with a smile. "That's how they could creep up on animals with their bows and arrows."

"We will follow you, O Great Warrior, and do whatever you do," Patrick laughed as he roughed Frank's hair and patted Chase on his muddy shoulder.

The closer the four of them got to the barbed-wire pen, the more commotion they heard. Two men were hollering, mostly with short phrases, whistles, and claps of their hands. When the Bon Air boys and Patrick reached a place that let them stay hidden but see the action, they understood why.

The trailer was backed up to the pen's opening, and two huge bulls were standing within the barbed-wire enclosure! Other animals appeared to still be in the trailer. From their size and near-perfect form, it was clear that these were prized blue-ribbon bulls. Their mooing and darting around in their new environment allowed the boys to whisper without being noticed.

"Cattle rustlers!" Patrick declared with hushed words. "Look at their hindquarters. They have different brands burned onto them. I'm ninety-nine percent certain that these bulls were stolen."

Just then, the taller of the men spoke. "This cattle gig is almost too easy. We can put a thousand dollars in our pockets in just one night."

The other man laughed and added his thoughts. "Yeah, and your cousin just looks the other way whenever we tell him to—and for only fifty-bucks a pop! He doesn't seem to care what's going on back here!"

"And we intend to keep it that way, too!" the first guy said with a smirk.

Patrick tapped all of the boys on their shoulders, and he pulled them gently as he stepped back from their vantage point. While the mooing and the conversation between the two men continued, the four of them quietly retreated toward the hidden gate. Patrick stopped when they were halfway to the perimeter road, and the others stepped close to him.

"We need to get the Sheriff out here as quickly as we can!" Patrick said. "Who knows how long these two will hang around or what they're planning to do next."

"They might have a buyer coming, and if that happens anytime soon, the evidence will be gone, too," Frank said.

"If you noticed, there was no water or feed for the bulls anywhere in the pen, so I don't imagine they'll be hanging around there for very long," Griff said.

"We could've tried to call my sister with my walkie-talkie," Frank offered, "but Kate won't have the spare radio turned on any longer. She's probably still with Mr. Rigsby."

"I have an idea to mess with those guys' plans," Chase said. "I'll show you when we get back to the gate."

The four hurried away from the pen as quietly as they could, and when they believed they were out of range to be heard, they began to jog to where they had entered the preserve. At the chain-link gate, Griff lifted it to let the others pass under it.

Chase walked over to the wooden camera base they had left behind days earlier. "Let's use these wickets that we pushed in the ground. We can wrap them around the chain-link part and twist them onto the two fence posts. The metal wicket is about as thick as the chainlink, so the men won't notice why the gate won't open without doing a lot of searching."

Frank began to laugh at the thought of their confusion. "And if their buyer shows up and tries to go into the preserve, he *for sure* won't be able to figure out what's going on!"

"You guys are something else," Patrick said with a chuckle. "Go ahead and do that, and *I* have one more idea that might make for an interesting time back there at the pen."

Chase, Griff, and Frank used the four wire wickets and secured the chain-link gate to the fence posts in ways that were almost impossible to notice. While they were busy doing that, Patrick lifted the bottom two feet of the gate and slipped back into the preserve unnoticed by the others and disappeared into the shade and trees.

Frank, Chase, and Griff finished twisting the wicket wires and a few minutes later Patrick returned. The boys lifted the lowest part of the gate as he belly-crawled back to the outside of the fence.

"You all noticed the wire that connected the battery box to the barbed wire pen? Well, their electric fence isn't electric anymore!" Patrick beamed with a satisfied smile. "I sneaked in without them seeing me and shut down their box of batteries. I'm guessing that it has gotten *pretty* interesting back there by the bulls without any electricity going to the fence charger! Animals can tell by sniffing the wire around the pen that the power has gotten turned off." The others began to laugh. "They won't be afraid of getting shocked now."

"Let's try to call my dad with Frank's walkie-talkie," Griff said as they crossed the road. "If he or one of his deputies are within the range of my radio, this cattle rustling operation will be shut down quickly."

Patrick opened the car's trunk, and Frank retrieved his two-way radio and handed it to Griff. "The deputies all monitor channel 19, so hopefully, we are close enough that somebody on patrol can hear us."

Griff extended the antenna, switched channels, pressed the transmit button, and said, "Calling Jeffers County Sheriff's office. Are any deputies hearing me? This is Griff Jenkins. Over."

Almost immediately, a man replied. "The person calling for a deputy, your signal is weak. I could only hear a few words. Can you move to a better position and try to call us again?"

Griff spun around and looked in all directions. "I need to get higher," he said, "either on the roof of the house or up into that tree over there." He pointed to a large elm tree fifty feet away and began to head in that direction. "These bottom branches are pretty high, so one of you guys will need to give me a boost if I'm going to climb it."

The three friends followed Griff to a suitable place under a sturdy branch. There, Patrick and Chase each interlocked the fingers of their hands and gave Griff two places for his sneakers to step onto. He tucked the walkie-talkie behind his belt, and Frank helped to steady him as he stepped onto the hands of Patrick and Chase so they could boost him upward. In no time at all, Griff had pulled himself into the tree and was seated on the lowest sturdy branch. Within another minute, he had climbed to its top. The three friends on the ground heard him speaking with the deputy, and within a couple of minutes, Griff dropped out of the tree and stood with Chase, Frank, and Patrick.

"I explained to Deputy Harris what we've discovered, and he said that he would contact my dad— that somebody would be here as soon as possible."

"Let's go around to the porch and wait for them to arrive," Patrick suggested.

They all went to the front of the damaged house and found places with a view. It only took a few minutes for the quiet scene across the road to change.

•••••••

What none of the four had been able to see or hear was the most recent activity that had taken place two hundred yards away inside the preserve. When the men opened the trailer's back doors and lowered the ramp to the ground, two of the stolen bulls walked out of the cattle trailer without any difficulty. After the boys left that area, the third bull ran out of the trailer and went into the pen with some extra coaxing. The fourth and last bull wasn't nearly as cooperative. In fact, he wasn't interested in going *anywhere* and certainly *not* into the barbed-wire pen. One of the men walked to the cab of the truck and removed a handheld electric cattle prod from the backseat. He reached through an opening along the side of the trailer and poked the bull in the shoulder with its five-thousand-volt jolt. Inside the trailer, the animal's reaction was immediate. The bull bucked and kicked a dent in the side wall of the trailer. He snorted and moaned, but he didn't leave.

The second man went to the opening at the back of the trailer, and he stood between its rear doors and the opened gate that led into the pen. That man whooped and clapped and then tossed a stick at the bull's backside while the first man poked the bull once more—*this time* with the highest power the cattle prod could offer: *ten thousand volts*!

The bull jerked, pawed the floor of the trailer, turned his head toward the second man and glared at him showing cold hate in his big eyes. Suddenly, the bull spun around in an angry, twisting move that brought all four legs into the air. In another instant, the bull was down the ramp, outside the trailer, and in hot pursuit of anyone in the area who walked on two legs!

Panic flooded the faces of the men, and they began to scatter. The other three bulls noticed the fleeing men and the fourth bull that was now running free among the trees. The first three bulls also saw the unguarded gate. They burst through the opening and joined the fourth bull, who was circling the truck and still fuming mad from the electric jolt.

The men had no safe place for their escape other than in the cab of the vehicle, so they ran to it. The fourth bull, the one who had been shocked, came alongside the passenger side of the truck with his head lowered just as the man pulled his door closed behind him.

With the might of two thousand pounds of meat and bone, the bull backed up and then crashed his head and horns into the door only inches below the window. The impact had such force that the window glass shattered, and inside the truck, the door handle, the interior door panel, and the window crank flew across the cab and landed on the floor!

The driver, his hands shaking almost uncontrollably, was finally able to pull the truck keys out of his pocket and start the engine. He pressed the accelerator to the floor, and at first, the truck's wheels spun helplessly on the damp ground. Finally, the tires found enough traction that the truck began to move forward with the trailer's rear doors swinging wildly and its ramp dragging on the ground.

Two of the first three bulls joined in the pursuit of the men, and the fourth bull made another running hit into the truck's cab. Another bull ran ahead of the truck and planted itself firmly between the truck and the gate.

That's when the Bon Air boys and Patrick first saw what had been going on. As the truck with its trailer slid to a stop only inches from the defiant bull, from across the road, the audience of Patrick and the three friends saw the terror in the eyes of the driver and the passenger.

The twelve-foot tall fence had sturdy posts that were anchored deep into concrete. The men in the truck realized they wouldn't be able to go around the bull and get out of the preserve. They also didn't know about the wire wickets the boys had twisted into place that made the chain-link gate stronger than ever!

The truck was within ten feet of the exit. The driver hesitated, considered his choices, blew the horn, and decided to attempt to push the bull aside. Unfortunately for the men, he waited a few seconds too late. Three of the bulls had lined up on the passenger side, and all of them lowered their heads at the same time. They pawed the ground with their enormous hooves, snorted loud enough to be heard by the boys on the porch, and proceeded to ram the truck and trailer with the force of three tons of raw muscle.

At first, the truck tipped halfway toward the driver's side, and it seemed to hang there as if it might remain at that awkward angle, frozen in space. That's when the final event seemed to happen in slow motion. The boys and Patrick watched as the truck began to lean ever so slowly, more and more, until it tipped entirely over and landed sideways on the ground. Following the same slow motion, but seconds later than the truck, the cattle trailer began to lean until it, too, fell onto its side. The bulls, appearing satisfied with this outcome, turned around, kicked up their heels, ran away from the fence, and were quickly gone from view into the trees.

Inside the cab, the men were piled together in a heap against the inside of the driver's door. Before they could unwind themselves from the tangle of arms and legs, two patrol cars, their sirens wailing and lights flashing, arrived from the Jeffers County Sheriff's Department. Chase, Patrick, Frank, and Griff, who had watched the rolling over from the porch, rose from their seats and walked to meet the officers.

Deputy Harris steered his cruiser onto the shoulder of the road and came to a stop directly in front of the gate and the sideways truck.

"Tell me what I'm looking at here," he said to Griff as he exited his car.

"I'd say it's a case of *men versus beef*—and *the beef won!*" Griff replied with a sheepish smile.

"All right then. Um, let me go check on the people in the truck," Deputy Harris said. "Your dad is two minutes behind me, and I'll let you tell him what all has happened here."

"You'll need some wire cutters," Chase suggested.

"I have some in my trunk," Patrick offered. "I'll get them and meet you at the fence."

•••••••

By the time Sheriff Lee Jenkins arrived and parked his patrol car, the men from the pickup truck had climbed through the broken passenger window and now stood atop the badly dented door. One of them had a cut above an eye, and the other was holding on to his limp arm from his tumble inside the cab when the truck turned over. They both searched anxiously around for any sign of the four-footed beasts. One of them hollered, "*Hurry up and open the gate before those monsters come back!*"

Once Deputy Harris, Patrick, and Chase lifted the chain-link gate, the two men slid down the hood of the truck, dropped to the ground, hurried under the gate, and walked directly to the waiting Sheriff Jenkins.

Griff leaned toward his dad and spoke into his ear. "These are bad guys, Dad. I believe they're Mr. Mueller and Mr. Boyd Abbott!" he said quietly.

130

"Okay, the first thing that's going to happen is we're going to drive you both to the infirmary and get you checked out. After that, I have some questions for you at my office," Lee Jenkins said. "My deputies will each take one of you and stay with you. And I'll expect to see both of you at the Sheriff's office as soon as the infirmary releases you."

"That Denton guy is in on this just as much as we are!" snarled Arnold Mueller.

The deputies seated both men in different vehicles. Before Deputy Harris closed the back door of his patrol car, the short man, Boyd Abbott shouted, *"We ain't taking the rap alone!"*

Once the two patrol cars had left, Lee Jenkins turned to Griff. "Now, suppose you begin by telling me what's going on here. How are you three—you *four*—involved in this?" He turned to the soldier. "And who are *you*, young man?" he asked of Patrick Wilson.

Griff stepped toward his dad and put his open palm gently on his father's chest. "Dad, I have wanted to tell you before today, and in fact, I *tried* a couple of times. First of all, this is Patrick Wilson. He's a soldier at Fort Everett, and he's the one who found Frank's dog Duke last Sunday."

For the next few minutes, the three boys brought the Sheriff up to date, relating to him all of the information they had learned, beginning with the voices Frank first heard on his parabolic microphone six days earlier.

When Griff finished his explanation, Lee Jenkins took a step back, scratched his head, and managed a half-smile. "I don't know if I'm upset or impressed, but I'm mostly glad that no one was seriously hurt." He looked at Chase's mud-caked jeans. "You, young man, were fortunate that nothing but mud was at the bottom of that pit trap!" The Sheriff then looked at Patrick and reached toward the young soldier. The two shook hands, and Lee Jenkins addressed him. "Thank you for looking after these boys so well, Patrick."

The Sheriff turned and walked to his car. "From here, I'm going to pay a visit to Mr. Denton. I have an idea that he'll cooperate with me now that Abbott and Mueller have been caught red-handed. And after that I need to get back to town and interrogate those two." He wagged his head, placed one hand atop his open door, and said, "I probably ought to hire all of you guys and put you on the payroll as my detectives. I would if I could." He slid into his seat, closed the door, and through his open window, he said, "Well done, men!"

Chapter 10

As Patrick and the three boys returned to Lewisville, they talked about the events of the past six days—the details Griff had told his father.

"That was a pretty sneaky system that Arnold Mueller had," Chase said. "He was the one who decided when the county workers mowed along the roads. As long as he kept the grass and weeds tall and overgrown on that one-mile stretch of the right of way, nobody would notice his truck and trailer tracks that led to their secret gate into the preserve."

"You're right about that," Frank agreed. "And when it was time to bring the stolen cattle onto the preserve property, or when they expected a buyer, they could just pay Mr. Denton a few dollars to keep the front gate locked. That way, nobody would be around on that day to hear the commotion of cattle coming or going. He was very happy not to know *too* much while he made some extra money."

"I wonder how long this cattle rustling has been going on. I had never hiked far enough into the preserve to come across their electric pen." Patrick commented.

"I wouldn't have a clue," Chase replied, "but by them adding electricity to the pen, it seems like they expected to be in business for a long time."

"The thing they didn't count on was Frank's super-duper hearing from his parabolic microphone," Griff said. "They thought they were just talking to each other on Sunday when we were there looking for birds. It turns out that their secrets weren't so secret after all!"

They passed the Town Limits sign and soon arrived at the Bon Air Village neighborhood.

"Would you mind dropping off Chase and Griff at their houses? Both of them live within a block of my house," Frank said to Patrick.

"I'll be glad to," he replied.

"Before you do that, Patrick, how about we all go by and visit with Mr. Rigsby for just a few minutes?" Griff asked. "I would love to tell him about us discovering the cattle rustlers and get another chance to look in his attic for whatever it was that someone broke in to try and find."

"That's right, guys," Chase agreed. "The deed to the preserve is probably up there—at least Mr. Rigsby thinks so. And he can't climb those steps to look for it—especially not anytime soon."

"Frank, you tell me again where to turn, and we'll all go visit him," Patrick offered.

"It's still a couple of hours before we normally eat supper, and my mom is cooking a special meal for you. So, yeah, let's head to Mr. Rigsby's house for now!" Frank said to Patrick.

Frank directed him to again park near the carriage house. Kate's car was in the driveway next to the house, so they walked to the back porch, up the steps, and stopped at the rear screen door.

"Knock-knock," Frank said. "May we come in?"

The back door was halfway open, and through the screen, Frank saw his sister headed toward them to welcome her brother and the others.

"Come in, come in!" Kate said. "I was just visiting with Mr. Rigsby before I warm up his supper." She looked at the boys and Patrick as they filed into the house. "Chase, your dad left about fifteen minutes ago, and while he was here, he replaced that broken glass pane in the back door."

Kate led them into the parlor, where Mr. Rigsby was seated in the same high-back chair, exactly where he had been when they saw him earlier.

"I don't think you'll have to worry about anyone else breaking your windows after today, Mr. Rigsby," Frank said. "The bad guys are either *already* caught or *about* to be caught."

Mr. Rigsby appeared confused, but then he smiled. "If you boys say so, I'll rest easier just knowing this."

Frank spent several minutes explaining their discoveries over the last six days. Leonard Rigsby was amazed and impressed with the Bon Air boys' detective skills, and he thanked them and Patrick for all of their work.

"The men will all be facing my dad for questioning at the Sheriff's office, probably at this very moment," Griff explained.

"Mr. Rigsby," Chase began, "we would like to look in your attic to see if we can find the missing deed. From what we understand, you think it's somewhere up there, but you just aren't sure where, correct?"

"That's right, Chase. I would be very grateful if you would search for it since I can't make that climb any longer. After my wife died, I hadn't had any reason to go into the attic. Honestly, there are so many things there that remind me of her and my daughter that at first, I simply avoided it. Nowadays, these old legs and my knees won't let me go up there without a lot of difficulties."

"We'll do it for you, Mr. Rigsby!" Frank said boldly. "If the deed is in the attic, we'll find it!"

They excused themselves and started up the broad staircase to the second floor. Frank led the way through the hallway to the door to take them to the top floor. He flipped a switch on the wall, and three bare light bulbs glowed brightly overhead along a wire that ran the length of the attic.

"How about we start at the four corners of the room, and everyone work their way back towards the center?" Griff suggested.

The other three nodded in agreement, and the search was underway. For the most part, Chase, Frank, Griff, and Patrick searched in silence. Once in a while, someone opened a box or removed a stack of letters that contained official-looking documents, and the others gathered to inspect the contents. But every time they examined the papers, the boys were disappointed.

Twenty minutes into their search, Patrick broke the silence. "Guys, come look at this!" In front of him were a half-dozen framed paintings that years earlier someone had leaned against the attic wall in a stack. One-by-one, he tilted them slightly forward to examine each painting. As the three boys gathered by Patrick, he lifted the fifth one—an oil painting mounted in an ornate gold frame. He turned the picture toward them.

"Does this place look familiar?" Patrick asked.

The artist had captured the scene of a sunny day with colorful flowers among the climbing vines that spread out on both sides of the iron gates of the preserve's entrance—the same double gate they had all used!

"It sure does!" Frank exclaimed. The others nodded in agreement.

"Bring that over here under a lightbulb," Griff suggested, "so we can see it better."

Chase helped Patrick lift the dusty oil painting over a steamer trunk and, from there, place it beneath the light from one of the overhead bulbs. In that location, its true beauty showed vividly.

"Turn it around," Frank suggested.

Patrick rotated it so that the unpainted side was now facing the boys.

"I see something there along the bottom edge on the back side," Chase said, pointing to a slight bulge in a corner.

"This frame has a false back—a second canvas!" Griff said excitedly. "The front one has been painted on, but this back one hasn't. Something—a *thin* something, like pieces of folded paper—is between them!"

Patrick pressed a finger against the center of the back canvas and then touched the corner. "There's no doubt about it! I feel some edges that are about the dimensions of an envelope between the front and the back!" he said with a smile.

"Let's take it downstairs and show Mr. Rigsby," Frank suggested.

Chase and Patrick held on to the frame—one of them carrying the top and the other gripping the bottom. Frank led the way, and Griff walked behind them.

As they came down the staircase, Mr. Rigsby caught sight of the boys and turned fully toward them. When he realized what they were carrying, his face brightened.

"That was one of Clara's favorite paintings. It hung in our oldest daughter's bedroom until Margaret left for college—I would guess that was forty-four or forty-five years ago! I had completely forgotten about it!"

"Mr. Rigsby," Frank began, "we don't want to get your hopes up, but we think something's been put between two canvases. Look!"

Patrick turned the painting around. In the bright light of the parlor, the slight thickness of whatever was in the corner on the backside was even more apparent!

"Kate, would you bring me a knife from the kitchen?" the elderly man asked.

"I have a penknife," Chase said, and he pulled it from his jeans pocket, unfolded the blade, and handed it to Mr. Rigsby.

He cut the back canvas, following the shape of the envelope and being very careful not to damage the front canvas, with its painted colorful flowers and gate. Mr. Rigsby removed three yellowed pages from the slit he had made and unfolded a signed and sealed document—*the deed to the preserve!*

"This is what I hoped to find, my friends! *Thank you!*" His emotions began to well up, and he paused briefly, unable to speak for several seconds. "I cannot say thank you enough!"

Patrick, Chase, Frank, and Griff nodded, and, at the exact same time, they all said, "You're welcome!"

Kate laughed at the four voices speaking those words in unison. "Have you guys ever thought about forming a quartet?" she asked with a chuckle.

Chase didn't skip a beat before he replied

sarcastically, "*No!* Have you ever listened to your brother try to sing? A trio, maybe, but *not* with him—*please!*"

Everyone in the room, including Frank, broke out in hearty laughter—laughter that lasted a very long time.

Epilogue

Arnold Mueller, the disgraced county employee, and Boyd Abbott, the first of two nephews of the late Clara Rigsby, were examined in the Infirmary. Attending doctors treated their cuts but found no serious sprains or broken bones. They only sustained a few minor scratches, presumably caused by their efforts to untangle themselves among the broken glass when their truck turned onto its side. They were transported in two patrol cars and kept in separate cells at the Sheriff's office. Lee Jenkins wanted to be sure that they would not have the opportunity to conspire to give false stories when he questioned them.

When Sheriff Jenkins confronted Mueller and Abbott with the facts that were told to him by Griff, Chase, and Frank, they both confessed to the crime of robbery—the theft of farm animals. They each admitted that they visited county fairs around the state and noticed the prized bulls and other cattle. They were especially aware of the ones that won blue ribbons and trophies, and they waited until the crowds left—usually in the middle of the night—to load them into a rented trailer and haul them away.

The two men established a network of buyers for the stolen cattle in other states. They claimed that the cattle pen inside the preserve had only been in operation for a few months. Mueller and Abbot paid a former convict to forge registration papers that made it appear the men were the legal owners of the cattle. Neither man could recall how many bulls and prize cows had been stolen and sold.

The other lazy nephew of Clara Rigsby was the caretaker of the preserve, Ernest Denton. Based on the description the boys had given to the Sheriff, he was brought into the office for questioning. He denied any knowledge of the theft of the bulls until he was presented with the receipt for the rental of the trailer—the one that rolled onto its side when the three bulls rammed it. The rental paperwork bore his signature and drivers license number but Mueller's home address since they were accomplices in the scheme. Denton had dropped that receipt while in Mr. Rigsby's attic searching for the deed to the preserve. Both Denton and Abbot concocted the plan to gain ownership of the preserve when an unscrupulous lawyer that Abbot had once met while in prison convinced them they both had a right to the land.

Mr. Rigsby did not want to press charges against Ernest Denton for breaking into his home.

At their trials in criminal court three months after their arrests, Mueller and Abbot, the two cattle rustlers, were sentenced to serve three years in the state prison. They were also required to pay punitive damages to the owners of the four most recent two thousand-pound prized bulls. The current value was determined by the amount they would bring in an auction of elite livestock—$6,000 each. The judge left the door open for other cattle owners to also make claims against them.

Ernest Denton was sentenced to six months in the county jail for being an accessory to the crimes.

The judge closed the case and expressed his thanks for the assistance and testimonies of the Bon Air boys.

AfterWords

In the final chapter, Griff reminded his friends what you and I had already learned: Frank's invention allowed him to hear the voices and words of the two cattle rustlers when those men thought no one else was around—that nobody was listening.

There are some special words used to describe God. We don't hear those words spoken about you and me or people we know because no human on earth has the characteristics and qualities of God. First, God is *omniscient*, and that means He knows everything. There isn't anything anywhere that God doesn't already know. He sees where we are and what we are doing. He knows what we're thinking, and He knows what we need.

Another big word that describes God is *omnipresent*. This means that God is everywhere at the same time. God is able to hear the prayers of a young girl in India whose mother is sick, AND He can give comfort to a boy who just lost his dog on the other side of the world. God is everywhere. Our minds sometimes have a hard time understanding this, but it is true. He is omnipresent.

Have you ever whispered a secret to a friend? Maybe you have been in a room by yourself and done something that no one else could possibly see or know. I can tell you for sure that God heard that secret, and He saw you through the walls and closed windows. We cannot hide anything from God.

The Bible confirms this in Luke chapter 8, verse 17,

where we read, *"For there is nothing hidden that will not be disclosed, and nothing concealed that will not be known or brought out into the open."*

Luke 12:3 says, *"What you have said in the dark will be heard in the daylight, and what you have whispered in the ear in the inner rooms will be proclaimed from the roofs."* These verses are reminders that all of us will give an account of what we have said and done.

But what about the things we say and do that are good words and good deeds? God knows them, too. They please Him, and those things will one day be blessings to you.

So always remember that God, the Creator of everything, is tuned in and aware of your thoughts, words, and actions—those that are hurtful and helpful!

The Secret Of Hickory Hill
Lights On Wildcat Mountain
Whispers In The Wind
Password To Meade Manor
Echoes From Creek Canyon
Up The Spiral Staircase
Cabin On Copperhead Cove
Footprints In The Attic

Watch for the next book in the
Bon Air Boys Adventure Series!

*Visit BonAirBoys.com often for the
latest news and information about
upcoming books.*

*All titles are available on
Amazon.com
as paperbacks and for Kindle*

*Thank you
Melinda Weller
and Andrew Preston
for your
faithful help in making
my books better.*

*The author also wishes to
give special thanks to
these talented friends:*

*James Bosarge
Jonah DeLange
Davis Tharp
Riley Chason
and
Nick Clark
Chris Cranton*

34,704 words